Natalie Jane Prior is the author of numerous
books, including the recent successful fantasy
series, *Lily Quench*, *The Paw*, which was an
Honour Book in the 1994 CBC Awards, and
the perennially popular *Bog Bodies*, *Mummies* and
Curious Corpses. She is also part-owner of a
business which imports and retails baroque
and renaissance woodwind instruments to
the Australasian market, and has a particular
interest in the baroque recorder.

Natalie lives in Brisbane with her husband
and daughter. When she gets a spare moment,
she enjoys sewing and gardening.

For Peter and Elizabeth

FIREWORKS
AND DARKNESS

NATALIE JANE PRIOR

Angus&Robertson
An imprint of HarperCollins*Publishers*

Angus&Robertson
An imprint of HarperCollins*Publishers*

First published in Australia in 2002
by HarperCollins*Publishers* Pty Ltd
ABN 36 009 913 517
A member of the HarperCollins*Publishers* (Australia) Pty Limited Group
www.harpercollins.com.au

Copyright © Natalie Jane Prior 2002

The right of Natalie Jane Prior to be identified as the moral rights author of
this work has been asserted by her in accordance with the *Copyright
Amendment (Moral Rights) Act 2000* (Cth).

HarperCollins*Publishers*
25 Ryde Road, Pymble, Sydney NSW 2073, Australia
31 View Road, Glenfield, Auckland 10, New Zealand
77–85 Fulham Palace Road, London W6 8JB, United Kingdom
Hazelton Lanes, 55 Avenue Road, Suite 2900, Toronto, Ontario, M5R 3L2
and 1995 Markham Road, Scarborough, Ontario, M1B 5M8, Canada
10 East 53rd Street, New York NY 10022, USA

National Library of Australia Cataloguing-in-publication data:

Prior, Natalie Jane, 1963–.
   Fireworks and darkness.
   ISBN 0 207 19971 X.
   I. Title.
A823.3

Maps of Ostermark and the city of Starberg illustrated by Linda Miller
Cover images by Getty Images
Designed by Lore Foye, HarperCollins Design Studio
Typeset by HarperCollins Design Studio in Sabon 11/15
Printed and bound in Australia by Griffin Press on
79gsm Bulky Paperback White

5 4 3 2 1   01 02 03 04

Genealogy of the Royal Family of Ostermark, 1712
and Governance of the Queen's Guard

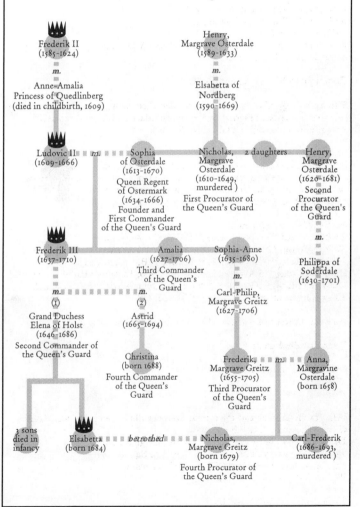

Frederik II (1585–1624)

m.

Anne-Amalia
Princess of Quedlinberg
(died in childbirth, 1609)

Henry,
Margrave Osterdale
(1589–1633)

m.

Elsabetta of
Nordberg
(1590–1669)

Ludovic II (1609–1666) m. Sophia
of Osterdale
(1613–1670)
Queen Regent
of Ostermark
(1634–1666)
Founder and
First Commander
of the Queen's Guard

Nicholas,
Margrave
Osterdale
(1610–1649,
murdered)
First Procurator of
the Queen's Guard

2 daughters

Henry,
Margrave
Osterdale
(1620–1681)
Second
Procurator
of the Queen's
Guard

Frederik III (1637–1710)

m.
①

Amalia
(1627–1706)
Third Commander
of the Queen's
Guard

m.
②

Sophia-Anne
(1635–1680)

m.

Carl-Philip,
Margrave Greitz
(1627–1706)

m.

Philippa of
Soderdale
(1630–1701)

Grand Duchess
Elena of Holst
(1646–1686)
Second Commander of
the Queen's Guard

Astrid
(1665–1694)

Christina
(born 1688)
Fourth Commander
of the Queen's
Guard

Frederik,
Margrave Greitz
(1655–1705)
Third Procurator
of the Queen's
Guard

m.

Anna,
Margravine
Osterdale
(born 1658)

3 sons
died in
infancy

Elsabetta (born 1684)

betrothed

Nicholas,
Margrave Greitz
(born 1679)
Fourth Procurator of
the Queen's Guard

Carl-Frederik
(1686–1693,
murdered)

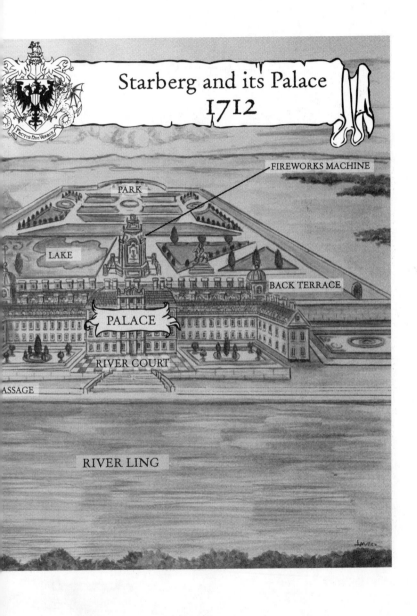

Starberg and its Palace
1712

FIREWORKS MACHINE

PARK

LAKE

BACK TERRACE

PALACE

RIVER COURT

ASSAGE

RIVER LING

BLACK MOUNTAINS

Nordland

Nordberg

Greiz

River Viska

Skelling

River Skelling

Osterfall

Osterdale

River Ling

River Dark Fosse

Starberg

Strasland

To North Sea

Pernt

River Ling

Soverdale

Frederiksberg

Lake Chadstin

The Kingdom of Ostermark
1712

At six o'clock precisely the lamplighter filled the lamp outside the firework shop at the end of Fish Lane, trimmed the wick, and set it alight. The oily flame glistened in the puddles in the gutter and picked up glints in the red and gold lettering above the door. *Simeon Runciman*, the writing read, *Master Firework Maker*. Through the open door the interior of the shop was a perpetual Christmas, alive with gold and silver paper and glowing with hoppers of stiff red crackers. Rockets hung in bunches from the ceiling, and behind the bottle panes in the tiny window was a toy cannon, a stuffed crocodile and the firework boy.

The firework boy was not usually to be found in Simeon's window. He was part of a firework display which had been commissioned for Queen Elsabetta's forthcoming marriage to her cousin, the Margrave Greitz, and was in the nature of an apprentice-piece. It was now seven years since Casimir had started working with his father, and, since it was generally acknowledged that this was the proper term to learn a trade, six months before his fourteenth birthday, Simeon had set him the challenge of making a set piece by himself. Casimir had made every firework from the coloured matches to the catherine wheels, to the red-skinned crackers that burst their skins like sausages on a fire, as well as the mechanism that would make the structure come to life when it was set alight. All this had taken him four months of working at night after the shop was closed, then there had been three days to cut the life-size shape out with a hacksaw and another four to drill the holes for the coloured matches which defined the features. Finally he had painted the boy's shirt and trousers red and blue and his hair and eyes dark brown. Casimir worked with fireworks every day and ordinarily he did not find them wonderful in the least, but for him the firework boy was the most remarkable thing in the shop. Whenever business was quiet, on the pretext of cleaning the windows, he could not resist going out into the street to look at him.

Ten minutes after the lamplighter had lit the last lamp and disappeared around the corner Casimir left the shop and locked the door. From force of habit, he paused to bang on the window, but this evening, since he was in a foul mood, he did not wait as he usually did to see the crocodile jump on its string. It was raining, he was running late for a display, and because the shop had been busy with the Christmas rush, he was having to miss his dinner.

'Sodding fireworks,' he muttered. 'And Ruth too, the stupid cow.'

Casimir hitched the rockets he carried a little higher on his shoulder, adjusted their oilcloth covering and set off down the street. He was a gangly boy with a wide mouth, hazel eyes and a shock of dark auburn hair that refused to stay in place when it was combed and dangled in his eyes when it was not. His colouring had been inherited from his mother, and Casimir hated it, for in Ostermark, where most people were light-haired, it made him look like an exotic bird that had somehow forgotten to fly away for the winter. He had actually been known to frighten people, emerging unexpectedly from the dark recesses at the back of the firework shop, and even Simeon, in one of his rare jokes, had once compared him to a human roman candle. Of late, as his father's notoriety continued to grow, being recognisable had been more of a trial than ever. Simeon was a poet, a philosopher, and had been a gunner in the Ostermark Royal Artillery before turning firework maker. In the distant past, before Casimir was born, he had also been a magician.

At the end of the street Casimir left the Scholars' Quarter, passed the cathedral, and turned towards the palace and the River Court. Lights burned in the windows of the government offices that clustered around the palace buildings, and because Queen Elsabetta was in residence the carriageway into the River Court was lined with guards, standing to attention like sodden bees in their black striped uniforms. Casimir produced his pass, which granted him entrance to the palace grounds, the River Court, and the treasurer's house. He handed it to the man on duty and was checked through, though the sergeant made him wait in the rain outside the sentry box, he supposed, out of spite for having to stand out in the weather himself.

At last the man stamped his pass and let him go. Casimir put the dripping piece of paper into his pocket and followed the cobbled sweep around to the back, where a long wide tunnel formed the mews and delivery entrance to the palace and the adjacent buildings. He made his way along the tunnel to the treasurer's house where he stopped and banged the knocker on the servants' door. Nobody answered. Casimir waited a moment longer, then pushed it open and went inside.

'Hello?'

A small page in livery was sitting on the passage floor, eating hot chestnuts from a paper. The smell wafted up with the steam: sharp and charcoaly, making Casimir's stomach lurch. He had eaten nothing since lunch, and since he was currently at a stage when everything he ate seemed to disappear into a bottomless pit, any food, any time, was welcome.

'Want some?'

'Thanks.' Casimir popped a nut into his mouth: it was hot, floury and as good as it was inexpressibly inadequate. 'Do you know where Simeon Runciman is?'

'I'll go and ask. Here, you can eat them, I've had enough.' The boy dusted his hands off on his breeches and disappeared along the corridor. Casimir leaned against the wall to wait, juggling the hot nuts in his hands. Noise and cooking smells wafted from the kitchen at the end of the passage and footmen in aprons hurried back and forth, preparing for the party that the Margravine Ruth Winterhalten, the treasurer's widowed daughter, was giving for a brace of her aristocratic and artistic friends. But the page did not return, and, after a while, when he had finished the nuts and no one seemed to show any interest in him, Casimir picked up his bundle and went to look for his father.

Casimir had never been welcomed at Ruth's house. On the rare occasions when he visited he usually found himself left to kick his heels in the kitchen while Simeon was entertained upstairs. Casimir knew Ruth liked to have Simeon as a lover to prove how daring she was, for his ideas were generally considered extreme, and his poetry difficult to understand. What Simeon saw in Ruth was harder to fathom. Since his father was not given to confidences Casimir knew he was unlikely to ever find out, but he was not averse to snooping around when the opportunity presented itself. Upstairs, he found his way into an entrance hall filled with mirrors and crimson draperies, a richly carpeted main staircase leading to the upper storeys, and a door opening onto a book-lined study. On one wall was a huge oil portrait of Queen Elsabetta and her half-sister, Princess Christina. The princess was guest of honour at this evening's gathering and Casimir, who had no particular opinion of royalty, particularly when it was making him miss his dinner, turned his back on her and stuck out his behind. As ill luck would have it, at that very moment a door opened to his left and out came a youngish woman in a brocade evening gown. She was thin, blonde, and of medium height, with slightly rounded shoulders. When she saw what Casimir was doing, her face set into an uncompromising frown.

'Casimir! You're late. Simeon's been waiting for you, where have you been?'

'Working. The shop doesn't close until six. It was busy and I couldn't get away.'

'Don't be ridiculous. All you've got to do is put a closed sign up and shut the door.' Casimir said nothing and she looked at him sourly. 'What are you doing upstairs with those rockets anyway? They're filthy, Casimir, and so are you; take them outside at once. No, not the main staircase. The back stairs. Down the corridor and turn left. Your father will be with you shortly.'

'Yes, ma'am.' Casimir shouldered his rockets and gave a mock salute. Then he went, not because Ruth had told him to, but because he knew that if her steward saw him there would be trouble. Deliberately or otherwise, he had forgotten to wipe his feet, and had left a trail of mud and water the entire length of the hall carpet.

⁂

Outside, Casimir crossed the mews, noting that a number of coaches had now arrived. The drivers were jostling for the best places in the stables, and their loud voices echoed in the enclosed space and followed him down the tunnel to the gate which led out into the grounds. Simeon had set up the bulk of their display earlier that afternoon in the park behind the palace, and the loaded firework mortars waited under cover a few hundred yards away across the squelchy grass. Casimir pulled back the canvas sheeting, unwrapped his rockets and set them ready for launching on the nails. It had stopped raining, but the mist was thickening on the ground and over the lake; and even in his leather coat and trousers his arms and legs were numb with cold. Casimir filled the fire buckets and checked the firework shells Simeon had loaded into the mortars. Then, with a glance at the sky, he dragged the canvas cover back over the lot.

It was a small, routine display, the sort Casimir and his father had put on hundreds of times for weddings, birthdays and festivals in towns all over Ostermark. Two weeks from tonight though, the park would be the scene of the greatest firework display Simeon had ever designed: a pyrotechnical extravaganza employing dozens of painters, carpenters and powder makers and costing a queen's ransom to mount. There would be a bonfire and thousands of fireworks, a waterfall streaming golden light, a winged horse which flew on a wire above the trees. In the clearing between the lake and the pine grove the queen's carpenters were building what Simeon called a firework machine, an enormous scaffold in the shape of an ornamental archway which would form the backdrop to the main part of the display. When lit, it would blazon the arms of Queen Elsabetta and her new husband in catherine wheels and coloured matches, while hundreds of white doves were released from the back through cascading showers of silver rain.

The trees would be filled with dragon lights and coloured lanterns. There would be musicians and conjurors and stalls selling hot food. The lake would swim with water-globes shaped like birds, letting off clouds of luminous, perfumed smoke. In the palace itself the festivities would last throughout the night. Ruth would be there as lady-in-waiting to Princess Christina, accompanied by her father the treasurer. Casimir supposed he should be grateful that Ruth had used her influence to get them the display, but he still hankered for the days when he and Simeon had roamed at will from city to city, and couldn't help wishing Ruth would refrain from interfering in every aspect of their lives.

A whistle sounded in the darkness to his left. Footsteps crunched on the gravel path and Casimir turned. A man holding a lantern was heading towards him. He was dressed in the black and yellow uniform of the Household Guard and carried a long double-pronged pike over his shoulder. The guard left the path and came over to where Casimir was standing.

'Papers, please.'

Casimir felt once more for his pass. The guard checked it over by the light of his lantern, made a mark on it with a pencil and handed it back to him. His breath made little clouds of vapour, like a dragon.

'Display tonight?'

'Yes,' said Casimir, and added, 'it's for Princess Christina. She'll be watching, up there, in the house.'

'I see.' The guard was unimpressed. 'What time do you plan to begin?'

'As soon as my father gets here. We're starting early because of the weather. You can watch if you like.'

'Sorry. I've got to be at the next checkpoint in seven minutes. But I'll look out for it over the trees. See you later, maybe.'

'See you,' said Casimir.

The guard picked up his lantern and went back to the path. Since Casimir had nothing else to occupy him, he stood for a moment following his passage through the darkness. The gravel path led past the lake and the half-built firework machine into a small grove of pine trees, and the whistling wafted back in snatches over the water. But as the guard neared the firework machine, something extraordinary happened which Casimir might not have credited, had he not in the past been witness to much stranger things.

As the guard's footsteps grew fainter, his whistle did not fade, but grew louder. The snatch of sound strengthened and the notes blurred into a single tone, like threads twisting into a cord. All the hairs prickled on the back of Casimir's neck and he shivered as if there had been a drop in temperature. A strange sensation rippled through his body and the scene before him contracted like a telescope, focussing his attention on a single point.

In the shadow of the firework machine stood a man. He was dressed in black with his dark hair tied back in a tail behind his head, and if it had not been for the pale smudges of his face, hands and bare feet, he would probably have been completely invisible. He was so still he might almost have been a part of the darkness. Casimir could not guess how long he had been standing there. It might have been a minute, or it might have been hours. There was nothing about him to say where he had come from, or why.

With every step the guard was drawing closer to him. Any moment now the two men would see each other and there would be a confrontation, perhaps a scuffle and an arrest. Casimir willed the intruder to withdraw into the shadows, but instead he stood his ground. The guard was almost on top of him, and now Casimir realised it was him, not the dark-haired man who was walking into an ambush. Casimir took a few steps forward and then started running towards the path. He yelled a warning, but his shouts stuck in his throat. The guard passed within an arm's length of the intruder and went whistling into the dark as if there was no one there at all.

Now the dark-haired man looked straight at Casimir. He made no attempt to speak or make any other contact, but as their eyes met every muscle in Casimir's body seemed to lock. His breath seized in his lungs and there was a jolt somewhere in his head, as if someone had opened a drawer in his mind and was rummaging through it. Thoughts, memories, images of his father and himself flashed through his head and evaporated. He saw his mother, his father in his gunner's uniform and in the firework shop; himself as a small boy, laughing and playing, getting gradually older and older until—

'Casimir!'

The drawer slammed shut. Casimir's mind went blank and he sagged and dropped to his knees as if suddenly released. For a few seconds of sheer panic he did not know who he was, or where, or what was happening. Then his sense of reality came trickling back. He was in the park behind the palace. A cold wind was blowing into his face. His hands were trembling and he was sweating all over, but when he tried to remember why, there did not seem to be a reason.

'Casimir. Are you all right?'

The voice sounded again behind him. Casimir turned. A thin man in a peaked hat and huge, caped, oilskin topcoat was hurrying towards him across the grass. Casimir stood up and wiped his hands on his trousers. The expression on his face must have told his father that something was wrong, for Simeon looked at him sharply and flared his nostrils as if scenting the air.

'What's the matter? What's happened?'

'I don't know. I just felt dizzy all of a sudden. Maybe I'm ill.'

Simeon narrowed his eyes. Casimir saw that he did not believe him. His father was about to say something else, but before he had a chance to speak, it started raining again. It was only a light drizzle, but it distracted Simeon's attention and he looked up at the clouds with an exclamation of disgust.

'That's finished it. We'll have to move quickly or we'll lose the whole display. Come on, Cas, give me a hand with this tarpaulin.' He grabbed a corner and started hauling it back, at the same time firing off a list of instructions. 'It's a standard set up. I'll work the rockets, you do the mortars. Five seconds between each flight, alternating rockets with shells. Then the silver fountains and the set piece with the catherine wheels.

Roman candles, more rockets, and the big shell with the loud salute last of all. That should impress them. With all this cloud cover to hold the noise in, it'll sound like doomsday. Have you got all that?'

Casimir nodded. He put some wax plugs into his ears and dragged his leather cap down over his fringe so it wouldn't catch fire. He was still not exactly sure what had happened on the path, but he was already forgetting about it. The display demanded his complete concentration; there was no time now to think about anything else.

Simeon shifted the safety lanterns which gave them enough light to see. Upstairs, the lamps in the treasurer's drawing room were going out. Curtains were held back and faces watched at the windows. It was the moment of anticipation that Casimir normally relished, but this evening something felt different. He lit his slow match at the firepot and walked over to the mortars. His legs moved jerkily and he wondered briefly if he really was coming down with something.

Simeon dropped to one knee beside the first volley of rockets.

'Ready?'

Casimir nodded. 'Ready.'

He crouched down by the firework mortar, waiting. Across from him, Simeon touched his slow match to the first fuse. It hissed into life and there was a jolt, a whizz and a streak of light as the bundle of rockets disappeared into the sky. Casimir counted five and touched off his mortar, stepping back neatly before it detonated. The familiar thud and whoosh of the shell and the little flash of heat from the exploding gunpowder reassured him a little. By the time he reached the second mortar, the first volley of rockets was already exploding overhead and he had forgotten there had been anything unusual about the evening at all.

Red, blue and green flares reflected in the puddles and a haze of smoke from the gunpowder drifted across the ground at their feet. Casimir and Simeon worked in and out along the lines of fireworks with practised rhythm, not bothering to look up, relying on the overhead sound and flash of the fireworks to tell them how the display was going. About a quarter of the mortars and rockets were refusing to ignite, resulting in a patchy show, and Casimir could sense Simeon's annoyance in the set of his shoulders and the intent way he applied himself to lighting the fuses. Once or twice he caught him glancing vexedly towards the house. Princess Christina had approved their warrant for her sister, Queen Elsabetta's wedding. To put on a thin display tonight was a poor advertisement for the marvels they had planned for two weeks' time.

Casimir launched his last mortar. He turned to the adjacent row of silver fountains and as he straightened, glanced casually out across the lake. For a split second he paused, his attention caught. Something was moving in the shadows underneath the half-built firework machine, something human, that should not have been there.

Suddenly, without warning, Casimir's body lurched out of control. One foot shot out and kicked over the firepot, coals flew out across the ground and skittered under his boots and the silver fountain he had been about to touch off toppled over with a crash on the ground. Casimir doubled over, then jackknifed backwards, spun around and started twitching from head to foot. Ignited by the upset firepot, fireworks started going off in crazy sequence around him. Some shot into the air, while others exploded on the ground or sizzed like lethal projectiles under his feet. Then the fountains ignited of their own accord, gushing silver fire like water from a hose, the salute exploded deafeningly in the mortar, and the catherine wheels came to life and whizzed around like demented miniature windmills, shooting sparks of red hot, blinding ash into the night.

Simeon yelled, but between his blocked ears and the noise of the exploding fireworks Casimir could not hear what he was saying. As suddenly as it had begun the strange palsy gripping him stopped, only to be replaced by a dragging sensation so strong it yanked him off his feet and dropped him into the mud. Against his will, Casimir spun around on his backside, flew up onto his feet again and started running away from the display in the direction of the firework machine.

'Help!' Casimir tried to shout but the word stuck in his throat. He hurtled across the gravel path and through the rushes on the edge of the lake, felt mud squelch under his boots and heard a waterhen flap out of the frozen reeds as he crashed up the opposite bank. A root tripped him and he fell, but the pull from the firework machine flipped him head over heels and back on his feet again. As he neared the scaffolding, a single rocket burst over his head. In its orange flare, in the shadow of the machine, Casimir again saw the dark-haired man.

His head was bowed in concentration and his bare feet were dug deep into the autumn leaf mould as if he were a tree drawing strength from the earth. Casimir ran right past him, so close he could feel the bristle of power which surrounded him. The firework machine loomed in front of him, but Casimir did not slow down. Instead he crashed straight into the scaffolding, scrambled onto it and started to climb. His arms and legs moved like machine pistons, splinters rammed into his fingers and palms and he felt a hot trickle of blood down one of his arms, but the force that propelled him was relentless and he did not, could not slow down.

Panic gripped him as he neared the top, but then, with only a few feet to go, Casimir stopped. All at once, every muscle in his body locked in place. Unblinking, unmoving, he hung there like one of Simeon's famous flying horses on a wire. The machine swayed precariously and a crossbeam snapped under his weight, but he could not have moved a fingertip to save himself.

Through the struts and angles of the scaffold he could see fireworks still exploding on the ground beside the lake, the dark-haired man standing waiting, watchful, and in control. As the last rocket exploded unnoticed somewhere above Casimir's head a second, smaller figure in an oilskin top coat and peaked hat joined him below. Casimir's father looked briefly upwards. He mouthed some words of encouragement which Casimir could not hear owing to the plugs in his ears, and then lifted his hand in an old, half-forgotten but still instinctive gesture.

An expression of intense concentration passed across Simeon's face. Very slowly a silver rope, like the children's fireworks that started out as a pellet and unfolded into a long ashen snake, emerged from the ground at the foot of the machine. The rope twined its way upwards through the struts and beams, moving surely towards Casimir like a vine climbing a trellis. It reached his feet and snaked tightly around his ankles. Then, gathering speed, it slid up around his legs to his waist. Finally it passed twice around his body and lashed itself to the scaffolding, securing Casimir in place.

Again Simeon looked up, as if checking his handiwork, and then he and the dark-haired man passed together into the shadow of the machine. Long minutes passed. At last Casimir saw them reappear, the stranger leading the way. Simeon was talking urgently as if trying to persuade him of something, but the other man was refusing to listen. Simeon grabbed his arm and he threw it off. The stranger turned, took a pace into the open and lifted his hand in a contemptuous, upflung gesture.

A flaming ball, brighter than any firework hurtled upwards and hit Casimir square in the face.

Casimir's head jerked backwards and he heard his neck snap. Everything went black and red and silver, the magic rope sizzled and dissolved, and he felt a disembodied wrench as his hands came away from the scaffolding. Then he toppled backwards from the machine. His body arced out into space, turning slowly over and over as if he were spiralling down through water. He felt his blood still in his veins, saw a grey mist descending, then heard, as if in the far distance, a shrill scream, suddenly cut off. There was an appalling thud as he hit the ground, then his body bounced and lay still.

I can't believe it, thought Casimir incredulously. I've been killed. Just like that. I'm dead and Simeon's let it happen. His father ran past, his oilskins whipping around his legs and Casimir felt a surge of anger that he should be wasting time chasing the dark-haired man when he was lying dead and broken on the ground. A cold sensation started slowly creeping down Casimir's spine. He wondered if this was what it felt like before everything went black for the final time, and then suddenly he realised the coldness was not death but damp, and that he was lying in a puddle. Casimir shifted his head gingerly and the loosened plug of wax fell out of his ear. He moved his foot and was startled to find it under his control.

Casimir slowly sat up. His hands bled and smarted when he flexed them and he felt giddy and disoriented, but amazingly, he was alive. Somehow, he had fallen fifty feet from the top of the firework machine and survived. Not by accident, though. Something or someone had absorbed the impact of his fall.

Lanterns swam in the smoke over the path and there was noise and shouting. Simeon came running back out of the trees.

'Don't say anything.' As he flicked past Casimir felt a crackle of electricity. There was something else too, a pungent smell which he recognised but could not immediately identify. His eyes lit on two objects lying in the mud beside him and he stared at them stupidly. Simeon's top boots. It was at that moment, with a lurch of fear, that Casimir remembered. The smell, the acrid unmistakable scent he had recognised from his earliest childhood was magic, lingering like gunpowder in Simeon's clothes.

'What's happened? Is he all right?' Ruth ran down the path towards them, her skirts bundled up around her knees.

'He's all right,' said Simeon. 'A rocket caught in the scaffolding. Casimir was trying to free it, but it exploded. Don't worry. He's not hurt. He landed in the soft mud at the edge of the lake.'

'*What?* How can—?'

'*He's all right,*' Simeon almost snarled, and she recoiled, wrinkling her nose at the stink of magic which clung to him. Casimir saw that Simeon was trembling. He looked faint and sick and there was a burn on his cheek where he had been caught by an exploding firework. Ruth was obviously not convinced by his explanation, but other people were arriving with a makeshift stretcher and she could not pursue the argument any further.

Casimir was bundled up in a blanket and a flask of brandy was thrust into his hand. He swigged it gratefully and then his legs gave way from delayed shock. Helping arms supported him and he was put on the stretcher and carried back to the house. At the foot of the garden steps he happened to glance back and see his father's face. It was white and utterly despairing. And at that moment, Casimir not only knew the dark-haired magician would be back, he realised Simeon was afraid.

CHAPTER TWO

Casimir woke next morning with a sore chest, stiff hands and a headache so severe it scarcely seemed worth his while getting up. Every muscle in his body felt as if it had been through a mangle. He opened his eyes, saw stars that had nothing to do with fireworks, and immediately groaned and pulled the covers back up over his head.

It could have been worse, of course. He could be, should be, dead.

After a while he heard the cathedral clock strike eight in the distance and realised he would have to get up. In half an hour it would be time to open the shop. Casimir hauled himself out of bed and dressed awkwardly. On his washstand was a folded piece of paper. It was inscribed in Simeon's handwriting ~for your head~ and contained a white, bitter powder which he tipped onto his tongue and swallowed. Like all Simeon's remedies it was effective. After five minutes, during which Casimir conducted his ritual morning search for facial hairs and found a record seventeen, he felt well enough to start the day.

Downstairs he found breakfast waiting for him: black coffee, fresh bread and porridge, slightly burnt after Simeon's fashion but still appetising with plenty of milk and honey. Casimir kept an ear open for his father while he ate, but there were no sounds of activity in either the workroom or the shop and he guessed Simeon had probably gone out. Casimir was not entirely sorry. He wanted to get the events of the previous night straight in his own head before he spoke to him. To do that, he needed to have time to himself.

Overnight, Casimir's memory of the attack had blurred. Only the shock of his fall and Simeon's unexpected response to it remained clear in his head, obsessing his thoughts with an awful inevitability. His return to Fish Lane had been scarcely less disconcerting. Casimir had endured an inhalation that made his eyes water, an infusion of herbs so acrid it made him vomit, and a violent purge that left him sick and shaking. He had gone out into the yard behind the shop and stripped naked while Simeon drenched him with icy water. Then, as if all this had not been enough to bear, he had been forced to stand there while Simeon paced around him, firing off a string of strange, seemingly irrelevant questions.

'What was your mother's name?

'Whose house did we just visit?

'How long since we opened the shop?

'Who is your master?

'The name of the waterfall with butter-coloured water?'

20

The interrogation went on and on, question after question, mindless and seemingly pointless, until Casimir was exhausted and almost dead from cold. At last Simeon seemed satisfied. He threw Casimir a blanket and let him inside again, took his pulse and made him stare into a candle flame while he scrutinised his pupils. Then he abruptly blew out the candle, gave Casimir a warm drink and a powder and told him to go to bed and get some sleep.

And that was it. No explanations, no apologies, no excuses, and Casimir knew he was unlikely ever to get any, even if he summoned up the courage to ask for them. He and Simeon had spent the last nine years almost constantly on the move, sharing all the vicissitudes and adventures circumstance had thrown them. Yet Simeon's past, and particularly anything that had happened before he joined the artillery at the age of eighteen remained, as it had always done, a forbidden subject. Even now Casimir did not know the names of his grandparents. He did not know where Simeon had been born, he did not know where, or even if he had gone to school. The one fact he did have—that his father had trained as a magician—he had found out by accident in the upheaval surrounding his mother's departure. The question of how the dark-haired man fitted into the piecemeal picture which was all Casimir had of his father's early life was one he was not entirely sure he wanted answered.

Casimir pushed aside his breakfast. The savour had gone from it and anyway, it was time to open the shop. There was no sign of Simeon, but since he was apt to come and go, the fact did not greatly concern him. Casimir wrapped a scarf around his neck and took his coat off the hook on the back of the door. Like the powder cellar and workroom the firework shop was unlit and unheated because of the risk to the gunpowder, but unlike Simeon, who walked around in his shirtsleeves regardless of the weather, Casimir loathed the cold. Working in the shop for any length of time was a penance, but so ingrained was his habit of caution that he felt almost guilty whenever he was warm there.

Casimir unlocked the till and the door and leaned past the firework boy to turn the sign in the window to *OPEN*. The bell on the shop door rang and with a flurry of closing umbrellas his first customers pushed in out of the rain.

※

Around lunchtime, Simeon came back. Casimir did not see him arrive. When the familiar footsteps sounded on the flagstones he was down in the powder cellar fetching rockets for a customer and by the time he came back up they had already turned into the workroom. A moment later a tap-tapping started up there. It was the sound of Simeon's driving hammer forcing gunpowder into newly made firework cases.

All afternoon the workroom door stayed closed, the sound of the hammer beating a relentless counter-rhythm to the rain outside. In his spare moments Casimir wondered where Simeon had been. Most likely, it was back to the park to salvage their gear, but there were other, more sinister possibilities he did not care to dwell on. At one point Casimir thought he saw two men in the black and red flashed uniforms of the Queen's Guard, standing in the laneway outside the shop. The prospect of this sinister fraternity expressing interest in their activities made Casimir almost dissolve in terror, but either he was mistaken, or the men had other business, for they soon went away and he did not see them again.

Outside the rain poured down, sending people hurrying in for shelter. The firework shop had gained a following among Starberg's well-to-do, and, with only a few days until Christmas, there was a steady turnover of cheap squibs and crackers. Casimir helped court ladies assemble huge orders for Christmas parties, served parents in search of presents, and did his best to keep youths his own age from leaving with pockets full of fireworks they had not paid for. It was not until nearly closing time that business finally slackened off. Casimir parcelled the deliveries and replenished the hoppers. As he worked, he noticed a lone boy standing outside the shop, looking at the crocodile in the window display.

He was soaking wet and must have been there for quite some time, but he made no attempt to come inside. From time to time he tapped on the glass to make the crocodile sway on its string, but otherwise he just stood, sheltering under the eaves, slouched up against their window frame with his hands in his pockets. Casimir willed him to go away. He knew

Simeon was strict about allowing people to loiter and that he would be irritated if no attempt was made to move him on. But the boy did not move an inch. When, after five minutes, he was still standing there, Casimir went over and opened the door.

'Can I help you?'

The boy looked at him. He was shorter, and probably a little younger than Casimir, with dark brown hair, a thin face and high cheekbones. His red and blue striped shirt and trousers had been cut down from a suit of men's clothing and his bare feet were so filthy they were almost black.

He jerked his head towards the window. 'The crocodile. Is it real?'

'Yes. It is real, but I'm sorry, it's not for sale. It belongs to my father.'

'I see.' At this point most people would have moved on, but the boy merely smiled at the crocodile as if he and it were old friends. Rain beat in through the shop door, pattering in little puddles between the flagstones. Casimir started to feel awkward and annoyed. He wanted to tell the boy the shop was closing, but any authority or sense of superiority he had felt was fast evaporating and he did not know how to say it.

'If you're looking for something in particular, come inside,' he said at last. 'Otherwise, maybe you should move on.'

'As a matter of fact I am looking for something,' the boy replied. 'Thanks. I'd like to come in very much.'

He stepped over the threshold. Casimir shut the door and turned the sign in the window to *CLOSED*. The light had faded and the shop was almost dark. A chill struck up from the flagstones underfoot and there was a firework smell of gunpowder, paint and glue.

The boy went to the very centre of the shop and stood, looking around him. His eyes took in the low ceiling, the bottle windows, the old apothecary's cabinet in which they kept fuses and matches. He looked at the closed trapdoor in the floor until Casimir was sure that if he had asked him, he would have been able to tell him everything that was stored in the powder cellar underneath. Finally his eyes fastened on the workroom door. Simeon's driving hammer was still tapping away inside. A strange expression came over the boy's face and his hands folded over at his sides.

'What can I help you with?' said Casimir loudly. 'The catherine wheels are a good buy. We reduced the price only this morning.' This was untrue, but the boy's staring was beginning to unnerve him. The sound of Casimir's voice seemed to break his concentration. He stopped looking at the workroom door and turned back to the counter.

'I'm not really looking for a catherine wheel. I'll have one of those big rockets. The ones with the stripes and the red labels.'

'They're expensive.' Casimir hesitated, but the expected query about the price was not forthcoming, so he fetched one down and wrapped it in waxed paper. 'Anything else?'

'A roman candle. A packet of squibs. And a pennyworth of small crackers.' The boy took some money out of his pocket. Casimir shook the crackers out into a screw of newspaper and cut a strip of slow match from the roll under the counter.

'Make sure you keep them out of the rain,' he said, with a sense of relief that the transaction was closing, 'and stand well back when you let them off.'

The boy saluted him with the rocket. 'See you soon.' The shop bell jangled loudly as he stepped into the street and he swaggered off jauntily through the rain.

※

'I went to visit Ruth this morning.' In the quiet of the deserted shop Simeon's voice sounded unnaturally loud. Casimir jumped and turned around. Simeon went on, 'She's a bit upset about what happened last night. It looks like there's going to be trouble.'

Casimir put the roll of slow match on the counter. His father was standing in the workroom doorway, an indistinct figure swathed with shadow. Outside, night had fallen. Rain drove in gusts along the cobbles. The lamplighter came and bobbed away again like a firefly in the gloom.

'What do you mean, trouble?'

'With the Queen's Guard. On account of Princess Christina being in the house when the explosion happened. They called Ruth up this morning to account for it, though of course, she couldn't tell them much. It seems we may lose the warrant. Well, I don't care about that, but we've borrowed money against it and it could become unpleasant if it's not paid back.'

'Did they speak to you, too?'

Simeon frowned. 'No. I thought that was rather strange. But the guard reports to Princess Christina and I'm to see her tomorrow morning. Ruth's arranged it for me.'

I bet she has, thought Casimir. He said, 'What did you tell her?'

'What do you mean?'

'I mean, did you tell Ruth about the magic?'

Simeon did not immediately answer. He ran his hand along the shelf at the back of the counter where they kept the coloured matches and roman candles. A phosphorescent gleam showed in the dust where his fingers had passed and when he took his hand away it left a small pale flame burning on the shelf behind it. Casimir felt something twist inside him. All at once it seemed there had been a fundamental shift in the mode of their existence. In the nine years since his mother left, he had never seen his father use magic, let alone so casually as this.

Simeon clicked his fingers. The flame snapped out.

'No,' he said. 'I haven't told her. But she suspects. She's not a fool.'

There was a silence. Words formed in Casimir's head, but fear blocked them on their way to his lips.

'Cas,' said Simeon quietly, 'I know what you're thinking. I know you're angry with me. But if there are things I haven't told you, it's for good reason. The magician who attacked you last night, Circastes, has been seeking me out for years. He holds a grudge against me and by extension against you. I've always taken the view that the less you know about him, the better.'

'Why?'

'Because of the way certain types of magic work. A magician can take the victim's knowledge, fears and desires and turn them back on him. When you know about him, you become frightened and your terror forms a link he can focus in on. The best protection is not to attract his attention in the first place.'

'But you're a magician, too.'

'Once. Not any more.'

'You used magic last night.'

'Only because Circastes let me. He gave me no choice. Neither of those things make it right.'

'You mean, it was wrong to save me? It would have been better to let me die?'

'No. I didn't say that, that's not the way it works. Cas, try and understand, this is not like anything you've ever experienced. I'm not talking about good and evil, black and white. When I say magic is wrong I mean something far more fundamental than that. Magic is interfering with the order of the universe.

'Listen to me. Imagine, at the beginning of the world, a book. A huge book, with the whole of creation written into it, full of instructions. Instructions telling the sun when to rise, instructions to hold the stars in their places. Instructions for the trees so they know when to fruit. And whole chapters, telling the story of the human race, a page for each man, woman and child who has ever lived.

'Magicians want to get hold of that book and rewrite the rules, but the problem is there's only so much they can rub out. They scratch out phrases and bits of sentences, and then try and concoct something that will fit into the gap. They try and force their own words into the spaces and the margins defining the page become ragged. Sometimes they're impatient and smudge whole sentences. At the very worst, when they try and erase the writing, the page tears across, and there's a hole which will never quite be fixed before the end of the world.

'Think of it Cas. That is the sort of power a magician wields. He creates nothing. He merely manipulates what is already in existence, balancing spell against spell, setting up ripples of disturbance, destroying to build anew in his own image. Let me tell you exactly what that means. It means that when you fell from the machine last night and I caught you, somewhere in the world, a boy your own age had to die. I don't know who he was, or where he lived, but his death was necessary to balance out the power I used to pervert the laws of nature and save you. I killed him, and his death will remain on my conscience, but men like Circastes *have* no conscience. They are trained to believe that all things and people are expendable to their purposes. I, too, once thought like that. That is why I gave up magic. *That* is why I know what Circastes does is wrong.'

Casimir said nothing. He was still standing behind the shop counter and Simeon was blocking his way out, but he suddenly found he wanted desperately to get out of the room. Simeon reached out a hand to his shoulder and he recoiled as if he had been struck.

'No! Don't!'

'Casimir, listen—'

'No!'

'Listen to me! This is important. Do you think I haven't spent the whole day chasing this round inside my head, wondering what to say? You're upset, Cas, but I have lived with this for twenty years—twenty years trying to be sure in my heart what is right and what is wrong.'

'How can you say that? How can you talk about what's right and wrong when you've just told me you killed someone?'

'Yes. I killed someone, but I did it to save you. There are worse things, Cas, far worse. That boy is dead and will never come back to life, but there are people walking on this earth who are dead inside because of what magicians like Circastes have done to them. A magician can turn you into another person without your knowing it. He can give you memories you never thought you had, he can take away your free will, change your character, make you do things you would normally never do. I know, Casimir, because I've done it. Not once, but many times. Sometimes I was even proud of it. But then I made a mistake. It wrecked my life, it wrecked your mother's, and now it's wrecking yours too and I don't know how to stop it.'

'What mistake? What did you do?'

'I looked into a grimoire, a book of spells,' said Simeon, 'when I was seventeen and in the last year of my apprenticeship. And I cast a spell, a stupid spell. It doesn't matter now what it was. The grimoires were all locked up, but my master was away from home, and I thought I was safe to pry. I was wrong.'

'What happened?'

'My master came home and caught me,' said Simeon. 'When he saw what I was doing he severed my indentures, ended my apprenticeship. You can't understand what that meant, Cas. When I was apprenticed to him, I was ten years old. It was my tenth birthday and every memory I had of my life before that day was wiped from my head. I couldn't remember my parents, I didn't know where I'd been born or who I was. I had to give my master the power of my name, so he could control whether I lived or died. For him, I had rejected the world, and now I had to go back out into it. The real world, a world I knew only dimly from the images in my crystal. A world without magic.

'You must understand: my master would never let me go without taking back all I had learned from him. He fetched one of the other grimoires, one that contained a spell to banish memory, the same he had used on me when I came to him. When he started to cast the spell I panicked, tried to deflect it. I don't know what I thought I was doing. It shouldn't have worked, he should have shielded himself. But he didn't.

'All I wanted to do was protect myself. But instead I turned the spell back. It hit my master and erased his whole mind—left it blank as a baby's. And my master, the man whose memories I destroyed, was Circastes's father.'

'Circastes's father?'

Simeon nodded. 'That's why he hates me. Of course, as soon as I realised what had happened I ran away. I travelled, ended up in Ostermark, and joined the army. I think I was hoping I'd be killed, but I wasn't. Then I met your mother and you were born. But all the while,

Circastes has been looking for me. Now he's found me, and worse, he's found my son. You see, Casimir, that's what he really wants. That's Circastes's revenge. My son, for his father.'

Now Casimir was really frightened. 'Me? He wants me?'

'Yes. That's why he came to me in the park.'

'But how can we stop him? What can we do?'

Simeon wiped his face with his hand. His muscles seemed to have sagged, making him look much older than he really was.

'Nothing,' he said. 'Nothing at all.'

'Can't we run away?'

'Yes,' said Simeon. 'We can run. Again and again and again and still he'll find us. I've been hiding from Peter Circastes almost all my adult life, Casimir. Perhaps the time has come to stop.

'But we can be careful. There are three ways a magician can get power over you, three things you must always watch for. The first is never to invite him into your home. The moment he crosses your threshold he has the power of hospitality over every member of the household. The second is never to share food with him. You've already done that Cas, otherwise he would never have been able to throw you off the machine. I'm not sure how it happened, but the link is broken and he can't use it again. Finally, whatever else you do, you must never give a magician power by giving him the power of your true name. There are lots of ways he can trick you, so you must be very careful. Don't forget, he can change his shape, become a woman, a child, even an animal. Tell me, did you notice Circastes's feet?'

Casimir thought. 'They were bare,' he said. 'The ground was icy and they must have been absolutely freezing, but he wasn't wearing any shoes.'

'There are types of magic,' said Simeon, 'which require the user to be in constant contact with the earth. It's a way of controlling the power which runs through your body when you cast a spell. Here, let me show you something.'

Simeon pulled off one of his boots and stripped off the sock. The sole of his foot was burnt as thoroughly as if he had stood on a red-hot griddle, and covered in blisters and blackened, peeling skin.

'I got that last night,' Simeon said, 'rescuing you. It's so long since I've used my magic my feet have softened. I've helped the healing along a little, otherwise I wouldn't even be able to walk today. You get used to it of course, but the more magic you work, the more powerful you become, the more important it is to maintain that contact with the earth. I'm explaining this, because from now on you'll have to be on your guard. Last night was simply a warning. As soon as you see or hear anything unusual, you're to come and tell me at once.'

'All right,' said Casimir. As he said this, something niggled at his memory. But the thought fled away and instead he asked, 'Do you ever want to go back to it?'

Simeon looked sad.

'For seven years of my life there was nothing else,' he said. 'If I believed I had one, I sometimes think I would give my soul.'

Casimir's sleep that night was broken and disturbed. The dead boy whom Simeon had murdered in his place ambushed his thoughts and kept him awake, and in his train came ghosts from his own more distant past. Casimir's mother, Jessica, had been gone so long he now could scarcely picture her; her absence, after his small child's grief had faded, had hardly mattered until Ruth had arrived to drive the first wedge between him and his father. But tonight, unaccountably, Casimir found himself thinking about her. She had been red-headed like himself, with freckles and a throaty laugh, and he had a fleeting recollection of her playing the guitar and getting him to dance on the kitchen table, whirling dangerously around until Simeon had intervened and plucked him off. He knew she had not tried to take him with her when she went. At times, he had bitterly resented this, and as he grew older had come to question what sort of woman could have walked out on a six-year-old child. Now, all Casimir could remember was the stink of magic which had filled the house on the night she had vanished. In the light of what had just happened to him, it was hard not to ask what sort of provocation had made her go.

He wanted answers, but Simeon was not going to give them. The outburst in the firework shop had been uncharacteristic, born of necessity and stress, and he knew better than to expect it would be repeated. He himself was too oppressed by the enormity of what had happened to him to initiate any further conversation. Death, particularly his own death, was something Casimir had never cared to think about. And yet, last night he had confronted and come within a hairsbreadth of his own mortality. Casimir was not sure he could even face Simeon in the morning, knowing what he had done to save him. He felt he no longer knew who his father was, and furthermore, which was worst of all, he realised he was afraid of him. Artilleryman, poet, firework maker, anarchist, magician—Simeon Runciman was nothing but a construct of all these things, a man made of tissue paper who floated away layer by layer as Casimir tried to grapple with the reality that lay underneath. The further he pursued this, the more his father slipped away, until at last Casimir began to wonder whether there was anything at the heart of him at all, or whether he was just a void, a great, black blank which could never be filled.

The sound of the rain driving down over their slate roof finally lulled Casimir into an uneasy sleep. It was past midnight when he was woken by the sound of heavy furniture being dragged about in the room below. The noise was coming from Simeon's study, the otherwise unused parlour at the front of the house where he kept the accounts and did his writing. Casimir got out of bed and retrieved his breeches from the floor. Out on the landing something glimmered in the darkness around the skylight.

Casimir pulled on his clothes; he felt frightened, but was growing too inured now to evidence of magical activity to hang back. He went out onto the landing, where the skylight was set into the low sloping ceiling, and traced his hands over its wooden frame. Arcane silver letters glowed around it, like snail tracks in the dark. There were no proper words and the text was punctuated with occult symbols he could not guess the meaning of. But there was enough of Simeon's distinctive, sloping handwriting to leave him in no doubt as to who had written them.

Casimir went softly downstairs. A lamp was burning in Simeon's study, and inside, he could see Simeon himself standing in front of the window. He had dragged aside their heavy travelling chest and was writing intently around the window frame with what looked like a pencil, but which Casimir realised was actually a thick short wand made out of some sort of dark wood. Silver letters flared into life at the passage of his hand, like firework messages across a scaffold: bright at first, then fading to the same glimmer as the ones on the skylight. A faint magical scent exuded from the window, redolent as gunpowder on the first night of the summer firework season.

Simeon finished writing. He flexed his fingers and laid down his wand, and then, although Casimir had not made a sound, he looked at him over his shoulder.

'Go to bed, Cas,' he said. 'There's nothing you can do. Just go back to bed.'

He turned back to the window, leaned his forehead against the glass and stood, looking out into the darkness. Casimir stepped back from the door and crept away up the stairs to his attic. Later, when he woke in the greyness of early morning, he remembered that he had dreamed, not of Simeon or the previous night's horrors, but of his mother, Jessica, and the night she had left when he was six years old. In his dream, he had been a child again and had cried as he and Simeon drove away in haste and darkness. In real life, he had not understood that his mother was no longer there and had thought they were leaving her behind. But in the dream Casimir had seen her once more and known her. Which only made his grief on waking the keener: that after so many years the only time he could truly recognise her face was in a nightmare.

The rain had eased slightly overnight but the skies over the city were still clouded when Casimir went downstairs. He found Simeon in the kitchen, a fire burning before him on the hearth. On the table were several stacks of paper and the tin box—an old gun case—which held their personal papers. As Casimir came into the room, Simeon picked up a pile of pamphlets and tipped it into the fire. They caught, the chemicals in the ink turning the flames virulent green and purple.

'What are you doing?'

'Burning things we need to get rid of.' Simeon poked up the fire and started thrusting the contents of the tin box into the grate. For a moment Casimir watched without really registering what he was doing. Then a familiar-looking paper grabbed his attention and he yelled and dived at the flames.

'Hey! Don't burn that. It's my birth certificate!'

'Sorry, Cas, it's got to go.' The certificate was gone in an instant, the wax seal popping and spitting sparks as it burned more slowly. It was followed by the lease documents for the shop, several agreements with local money lenders, and the big stiff parchment that was their warrant for the queen's wedding. It did not burn, but curled up at the edges and smoked, like something still partly alive. Casimir stared at it, half fascinated, half horrified by the wanton destruction.

'Why are you doing this?'

Simeon did not immediately reply. He picked up his army discharge paper and read it over. Then he folded it up and put it into his pocket as if he thought he was going to need it.

'Because I've changed my mind,' he said, and for the first time since the attack in the park, his voice sounded normal. 'I think we should get out. Leave Starberg, leave Ostermark. If we can get to the coast we can take a ship. We can't take all this stuff with us, so it has to be destroyed.'

Casimir sat down. The reply was so unexpected he found himself catching his breath, but his initial rush of fear at the thought of venturing into the unknown was quickly followed by excitement that they were finally moving on. What about Ruth? he wanted to ask. He couldn't imagine taking her with them, but nor could he imagine her letting Simeon leave without a protest. Instead, he asked, 'What about the warrant?'

Simeon shrugged. 'They'll have the fireworks. A lot of the stuff we've made for the wedding is already in storage under the treasurer's stables and there's the contents of the shop. They're worth a fair bit. We'll have to travel very light, cover a long distance quickly. We'll leave tonight, after the curfew.'

No mention of Ruth at all. Casimir nodded. He knew better than to ask where they were ultimately headed, but for the moment he didn't really care. A fierce elation filled him at the prospect that, after nine months of Ruth's petty slights and humiliations, he was finally going to be rid of her. Meanwhile Simeon resumed his *auto da fé*, burning letters, bills, notebooks, and the rough drafts of poems he had written since their arrival in the city. Disposing of most of these did not seem to bother him, but when he reached his fair copies something inside him seemed to crack.

'Ah, no, Cas, not *The Tyrant*. I can't do that, it's like burning my child. We'll leave it for Ruth. She wrote it out for me, poor girl, it's the only complete copy.' His fingers, rough and blackened with ingrained gunpowder, curled possessively around the sheaf of paper and he set it gently aside. The last inconsequential items went into the fire, and then there was a loud knock at the shop door which made both of them jerk up their heads.

'Who's that?'

On a Sunday morning, there was no good reason why it should be anyone. Casimir looked at Simeon, who lifted a finger to his lips, and then the knocking sounded again, this time louder and more imperious.

'I'll go.' Casimir started towards the door, but Simeon shook his head. He stood up and went swiftly down the corridor to the shop. On winter mornings its north-facing interior was dark, and, if one was careful, it was possible to see out into street without being observed from outside. A few moments passed, during which all sorts of horrible possibilities raced through Casimir's thoughts. Then Simeon reappeared, shaking his head.

'It's Tycho.'

'Tycho? What does he want?'

'The philosopher's stone? The Holy Grail? Your guess is as good as mine, and you'll have to deal with it because I'm due to see Princess Christina in fifteen minutes.' Simeon grinned and started pulling on his coat. It was his best dark red one, but still seemed hardly grand enough for an audience with royalty. 'Put your mind to it and I'm sure you'll be able to get rid of him. Eventually.'

'Hey! You can't leave me! It's not fair!'

'Who told you life was fair? Not me. Don't worry, I'm sure the experience will be character building.' Simeon flicked his hair out under his collar and straightened his neckcloth. 'How do I look? Like a courtier?'

'Like a firework maker in his best shirt.'

'As it should be. And even the shirt has a hole in it.' The knocking started up again, and Simeon added soberly, 'Just get rid of him, Cas. Find out what he wants and send him on his way. And just in case. . . remember what I said last night. Don't invite him across the threshold and don't offer him any food.'

The warning sank like a stone into Casimir's fragile calm. As Simeon went out the door, he paused and poked his head back inside. 'Have fun.'

※

Casimir waited until Simeon had exited the yard door and counted twenty before he went out to the shop. He was rather hoping that by the time he reached the door, Tycho would have given up and left, but something must have alerted him to the fact someone was home. The knocking redoubled its ferocity until a voice from one of the neighbouring houses yelled out to him to shut up. A furious interchange followed. Casimir could not catch the exact words, but they were not polite. He only wished he had the courage to say as much himself.

Tycho was Ruth's cousin. At least, that was how Casimir interpreted the relationship. In reality it was rather vaguer than that, and he was not in fact sure whether Tycho was really related to Ruth's dead husband. If not for ties of blood or marriage, it would be hard to explain the friendship which existed between them. Unlike Ruth, whom even Casimir was prepared to admit was highly intelligent, Tycho was as stupid as he was self-opinionated. The master of the grand gesture, the fervent word, and totally lacking in common sense, he had not even the saving grace of being likeable. Simeon despised him, considered him dangerous, and had never gone out of his way to conceal this opinion. To his father's assessment, Casimir added an additional, personal grudge. Some nine or ten months since, it had been Tycho who introduced his father to Ruth.

Over the last few months, Casimir had often reflected on how their lives might have turned out if Simeon had not gone to Will Thursday's printery on that chill March Saturday afternoon. No doubt, he and his father would have moved on in their usual way, and there would be no firework shop, no warrant, and—disturbing thought—no Circastes either. But Simeon had gone there the week before they were due to leave Starberg, taking with him several recently written poems and the recommendation of Casimir's maternal uncle, Joachim Leibnitz. Tycho had chanced to be in the shop and, after Simeon had left, he had badgered the Thursdays to let him show the poems to his cousin. Since the margravine was known to be a woman of taste and influence, they had agreed, and the result had been a personal invitation from Ruth to attend a small gathering of her friends. Simeon had first refused, then changed his mind. Somebody had told him the treasurer's daughter was notorious for her opinions, and that only the friendship and patronage of Princess Christina kept her a step ahead of the Queen's Guard. So, against his better judgment, he had gone to the treasurer's house, and within weeks he and Ruth were inseparable. Casimir could still not understand what attraction she held for him. He knew little about sex, though he often thought about it, and even less about love; but he understood instinctively that their relationship was both complex and binding. His own experience could not compass it, nor explain the sudden flowering of work which had resulted, over the course of the short summer and autumn in his father's long poem *The Tyrant*. All Casimir knew was that he bitterly resented it, and wished Ruth and all she represented consigned to perdition.

Which made it all the stranger—now he had a chance to think about it—that Simeon was proposing to leave her without even saying goodbye.

Tycho was standing on the footpath, peering in through the window. He was dressed self-consciously in a velvet suit, top boots, a white shirt that flopped open at the neck, and a hat with a feather that made him look as if he should be sitting in a tree. The woman next door was still shrieking abuse at him. Tycho yelled back to her: he certainly knew, thought Casimir, how to make himself inconspicuous. He fetched the big key from under the counter and put it in the lock. As he did, he looked at the firework boy and felt a pang of disappointment. The emotion was trivially ignoble in the face of their many troubles, but after so much work, he could not help feeling sorry his apprentice piece was going to have to be left behind.

Casimir turned the key and opened the door. 'Can I help?'

His neighbour leaned out of her window. 'Yes. You can tell this turd to heave his filthy carcase off my doorstep.'

Tycho returned the pleasantry. 'Shut up, trull.'

'Shut up? Shut up? Who was it came banging on my door at seven o'clock on a Sunday morning?' yelled the woman. She leaned out of the window and Casimir hastily stepped back; fortunately, all she did was make a rude hand sign and slam the casement, leaving Tycho with his mouth half open on the brink of another retort. He remembered Simeon's verdict. 'Dangerous. He flaps his mouth like a fool and thinks his connections will protect him. One day he's going to go too far.' Casimir was inclined to think that anyone who dressed like that had already gone quite far enough.

Now he redirected his attention to Casimir. 'Is your father home?'

'No.'

'I need to give him a message.' Tycho looked impatient. 'Are you planning to leave me standing here in the cold, or are you going to ask me in?'

'It depends what you want. I told you, Simeon's not at home.' It occurred to Casimir that the injunction on inviting people over the threshold was highly inconvenient, but in this instance at least, their visitor was not Circastes in disguise. When Casimir made no effort to show him in, Tycho swore, pushed past him into the shop and stood there, alternately rubbing his hands and blowing on them. Casimir followed him in and shut the door.

'Damn cold in here. Don't you have proper heating?'

'We only light fires for cooking. It's too dangerous. There's enough fireworks here to blow up every building between here and the cathedral.'

'Really?' For a brief moment, Tycho looked interested. Then he seemed to remember who Casimir was and why he was there. 'Where's your father?'

Casimir considered. As Simeon was so fond of reminding him, in Ostermark, a careless remark might easily be turned against one. In the end, he just shrugged and said, 'I don't know.'

'The Queen's Guard haven't got him, have they?' The unexpected shrewdness of this question took Casimir aback, and he wondered what Tycho had heard. He shook his head, and Tycho went on, 'Ruth told me about that business in the park. Very interesting, particularly with Christina being there. Really made me think.'

'That must be a new sensation for you,' said Casimir nastily, and Tycho gave him a dirty look. He put his hand into his sleeve and pulled out a letter.

'For your father. Make sure he gets it, nobody else.'

Casimir took the letter. There was nothing on it to say where it was from, and the seal was merely a blob of wax with a thumb mark in it. Even the paper looked dirty and disreputable. 'What is it?'

'None of your business. Just keep it safe and give it to your father as soon as he comes home. That is, if he really is out.' Tycho glanced at the workroom door, as if he suspected Simeon was hiding from him. Nettled, Casimir opened his mouth to object, then remembered what Simeon had said about getting rid of him quickly. He started moving to the door.

'Don't worry, I'll give it to him when he comes back.'

He opened the door and Tycho stepped out into the street. As he did, the contents of an almost full chamber pot hit the ground inches away from him.

It had started raining again. Casimir stood in the doorway, watching Tycho walk off with an air of displeasure through the drizzle. When he turned the corner at the end of the street, a man came out of a doorway and followed him. Or so Casimir thought. Then the rain started coming down in earnest again, and he was no longer able to be sure.

※

Casimir went back inside and put Tycho's letter on the shelf behind the counter. He would give it to Simeon when he came home, but was under no illusions as to what he would probably do with it. Tycho fancied himself as a revolutionary and was constantly frustrated when others failed to rise at his call: he put into writing what sensible folk would not have dared whisper in their most private moments. Most of Ruth's friends considered him a joke, but one around whom it was best to be circumspect. Everyone knew Tycho was headed for a fall. The best thing to do with his correspondence was to destroy it.

Meanwhile, he had to get rid of the mess on their doorstep. Casimir fetched a pail of water from the butt in the yard and started flushing it over the cobbles into the central gutter. He was assiduously applying himself to the removal of a particularly large fragment from under their door scraper when a voice said,

'Casimir Runciman?'

Casimir straightened slowly. For a second, the denial was actually in his mouth. It was automatic, but even he knew one did not lie to a member of the Queen's Guard. The man was short-haired, young, and, despite the uniform with its red flashings, did not look unpleasant. Casimir nodded warily and he handed him a folded piece of paper.

'A summons from Her Royal Highness, the Princess Christina,' he said. 'You're wanted for an audience at the palace.'

Casimir had never seen Princess Christina. He had of course, heard a great deal about her. He knew she was Queen Elsabetta's younger half-sister and heir to the throne, and that, following her mother's disgrace, she had spent most of her life in distant Osterfall. He knew she was reputed to be highly intelligent, and that certain of Ruth's acquaintance were enthusiastic about the supposed progressiveness of her politics. He also knew she employed Ruth, an acquaintance from her Osterfall days, as a sometime lady-in-waiting. None of this, however, explained why she should want to see him.

On his arrival at the palace Casimir was handed over first to a footman, then to a gentleman usher who clearly considered himself too important to be playing escort to a grubby youth. He scarcely spoke, except to tell Casimir to change into a clean shirt and coat which he supplied from a clothes chest, and how to bow to and address the princess when he met her. Then he took Casimir down what was clearly the back corridor to the princess's apartments. The passage walls and floors were plain white plaster and scrubbed pine, and the only people on view were servants; having expected richly dressed courtiers and degenerate opulence Casimir was vaguely disappointed. At the end of the passage they went up some stairs into an anteroom. A second, more ornate door connected it to a bigger chamber from which emanated low conversational rumbles.

A woman was speaking, too indistinctly for Casimir to make out the words, and then a man interjected, his voice slightly, but indefinably accented. With a mild shock, Casimir realised it was Simeon. He strained to hear, without looking too obviously like an eavesdropper, but before he could make much sense of the conversation Simeon was cut off in mid-sentence by a second woman. This time, Casimir had no difficulty in understanding what was said, for the voice was authoritative and sharply raised.

'Please do not make any more excuses, Mr Runciman. I am not ignorant of these matters, nor do I appreciate being lied to. What I want now is your assurance that such an attack will not happen again.' Again Simeon spoke, more or less inaudibly, and the woman replied, 'Your resignation should not be necessary. It would arouse suspicion and make our situation even more difficult than it is already. Also, since it would undoubtedly ruin your reputation in Starberg, I cannot help wondering what your motives are in tendering it. If you are thinking of walking away from this, let me assure you, the Queen's Guard has a very long reach.'

Several minutes of further conversation followed about security in the royal park. Patrols would be doubled until the wedding was over and the firework machine placed under twenty-four hour guard. Finally, Casimir heard the tinkle of a bell and muffled footsteps as Simeon and, he presumed, Ruth, were shown out of the room through another door. His own usher went over and tapped discreetly on the anteroom door. A voice called out, 'Enter!'.

The usher went in and reappeared a moment later with a disgruntled look on his face.

'You're to go in alone. Remember what I told you about how to bow.' Casimir felt a surge of panic, then suddenly the door was shutting behind him and he was standing in a room unlike anything he had ever seen in his life.

It was not so big as he had expected. Casimir had imagined a huge space, but the princess's office was not even as large as Ruth's father's study, though like it, this room was filled with books. What was singular about it was its shape, which was perfectly round, and its decoration, which even Casimir, with his limited experience of such things, could see was exquisite. The walls, or those parts of them not lined with gilded book cabinets, were covered with gold and green *trompe l'oeil* work; there was a rich rose-patterned carpet, and a huge curved window, draped with soft velvet curtains, which looked out over the park. In the distance Casimir glimpsed the firework machine. Its top was blackened and listing slightly to one side. Evidently, they were in the south tower, the strange, turret-shaped structure which had been built as a retreat for his young second wife by the late king, Frederik.

The young queen—Christina's mother, Astrid—had died mysteriously twenty years ago; it was generally believed in the city she had been murdered by the Procurator of the Queen's Guard for taking one or possibly several lovers, and that the turret was haunted. If so, her ghost did not seem to trouble her daughter. Princess Christina sat now at a desk under the window, writing swiftly on a piece of paper. Mountains of documents were piled in front of her. Casimir stood awkwardly on the edge of the carpet, wondering how long it was going to take for her to notice him, and whether he should do anything to attract her attention.

'Wait there,' said the princess without looking up, and Casimir waited, wondering whether he should bow now, or whether, as the son of a self-confessed anarchist, it was appropriate for him to bow at all. The princess finished writing and laid down her pen; she turned in her chair, and, for the first time, Casimir was able to get a proper look at her face. His first impression was that, like her portrait in the treasurer's entrance hall, she was very beautiful. The princess's features were neat and flowerlike and her eyes very round and blue; her hair, like most people's in Ostermark, was straight and honey fair, worn swept back over her ears in smooth waves. She wore no jewellery except a pair of pearl earrings, and a golden bracelet which gleamed against the shot silk of her gown. Otherwise, the most distinctive thing about her was her perfume, which was rich and floral but, like her beauty, stopped short of being cloying.

'You are supposed to bow,' said the princess coldly, and Casimir went hastily down on his knee and bent his head the way he had been shown. 'I see you have not been properly instructed. Never mind, we will pass over it this time. Stand up, Casimir Runciman. I want to talk to you.'

She indicated a spot about three feet away from where she was sitting. Casimir approached uncomfortably. The princess got up from her desk and went over to a side table where a silver pot was keeping warm over a spirit lamp. She poured herself a tiny cup of strong black coffee and laid a delicate biscuit on the fluted saucer. Then, when she had stirred her coffee, she returned to her seat.

'So,' she said. 'Our problem is this: your father, whose politics are regarded as unsound to say the least, and who has the added handicap of being a foreigner in Ostermark, has involved us in what is apparently a personal vendetta. He has laid crown property open to an attack by magic, in which you, his son, nearly died. He also tried to lie to me about it, which, since he escaped arrest by the Queen's Guard only on my personal intervention, I consider not only an affront but a dangerous impertinence. How long he remains free is, I imagine, entirely dependent on the outcome of whatever investigations the procurator has ordered. The question I must ask now is how much you know about this.'

Casimir felt his face drain white. He should, he knew, have expected this, but when the guard had come to collect him he had somehow assumed that Simeon would also be present. Now he did not know what to say. It was hard to be sure how much it was safe to admit to, and how much Simeon himself had already told the princess. Casimir guessed he had tried to fob her off with the story he had told Ruth on the night of the display, that it had all been an unfortunate accident. If so, the ploy had obviously failed. The princess knew enough to recognise magic when she saw it, and Casimir knew too, that she would be intelligent enough to realise if he lied to her.

'Your silence already tells me you know quite a lot,' said the princess after a few moments had passed. 'Casimir, before you start trying to make excuses for your father, I think it might be helpful if you recognised the degree to which our interests overlap. Your father wants to protect you from further attack. I want to make sure Her Majesty's wedding passes off safely and without incident. Perhaps you should reflect on this and also remember that I have considerable resources at my command which might be of help.'

Casimir nodded mutely. For a moment the princess waited as if expecting him to say something, but he did not. In the end, she was the one who broke the silence.

'You may have some coffee if you wish. When you have poured it, sit down over there.'

She pointed to a small, uncomfortable chair. Casimir went to the side table and clumsily poured some coffee with his bandaged hands. He didn't really want it, but there seemed no polite way of refusing. He looked for milk or cream but there was none on the table, so instead he slopped three spoons of sugar into the porcelain cup, and then realised he had stirred it with the spoon from the sugar basin. Casimir laid the wet spoon awkwardly on the tablecloth and took two tiny biscuits. The cup rattled in the saucer as he went to sit down.

'Good,' said Princess Christina. 'Now that you are comfortable, I think it might be best if I explained myself directly. My dilemma is this. I could go to Her Majesty and tell her a security risk has arisen regarding the wedding, but she is very busy, and there is not a single shred of proof that this man Circastes is any threat to her at all. Alternatively, I could cancel your father's warrant. That would leave us without a firework display, which would be a disappointment; it would ruin him and you, and it would also reflect badly on me since I was the one who assigned the warrant in the first place. I need hardly tell you there were plenty of people who were against my granting it to a foreigner with a dubious reputation such as your father's. On the other hand, if I do nothing at all and Margrave Greitz, as procurator, subsequently finds out that there is a risk, my position is going to be extremely awkward. My future brother-in-law learned to hate me when we were still children. Our mothers were enemies. He also resents the fact that my aunt, Princess Amalia, bequeathed command of the Guard to me instead of to my sister. So, tell me, Casimir. Do you think there is any threat?'

Casimir hesitated. 'Simeon doesn't think so.'

'No, he doesn't,' said Princess Christina. 'But Margravine Winterhalten doesn't agree with him. I can see she's very worried. You don't like her, do you? I know

54

she can be irritating. But she is also extremely intelligent, so neither can I entirely dismiss what she says.'

'I don't think Circastes can be a threat to Her Majesty,' said Casimir firmly. 'Simeon told me it was a personal grudge between the two of them. I don't see how what's happening can be a danger to anyone but him and me.'

'No?' The princess sipped her coffee, and Casimir politely followed suit. 'But I'm afraid I can. Tell me, Casimir. Is your father a magician, too?'

The coffee was strong as medicine, and so hot it burned Casimir's mouth. Hastily he picked up the biscuit and bit into it, but it was marzipan, which he hated, and since he couldn't spit it out, he forced himself to swallow it. The princess watched him over the rim of her own cup as if she were following its passage down his throat.

'There's no need to look so alarmed, Casimir,' she said. 'I'm not accusing your father of anything. But on the other hand, you must know that there are laws against this sort of thing. Magic is still a proscribed act; we may not have burned any magicians in the last fifty years, but it's an old fear, and there are plenty of people who would do it if they had the chance. I am also aware of your father's political opinions. You'd be surprised what he's said to my face. He's told me he doesn't believe in governments and that we should all be ruled by nothing more than our consciences. He also hopes that, one day, these dreams will become reality. And of course there is nothing wrong with his having these opinions, as long as they remain only that—opinions.

So tell me, Casimir. Have you any reason to suspect otherwise?'

'No!' cried Casimir. 'No. He's never done anything, I promise you.' In his anxiety he almost spilled his coffee. The princess looked at him with surprised blue eyes.

'I'm glad to hear it,' she said. 'Please calm down, Casimir. You won't help anyone by becoming hysterical, your father least of all. But to return to the subject. I need hardly tell you your father has acted strangely, both at Friday's firework display and just now during our interview?' She paused. 'I see you realise he has. It makes me concerned that this man Circastes could. . . influence him. In that case, it would be up to you to come to me so I could help him. Do you take my meaning, Casimir? Don't pretend you don't understand. You know these things can happen, don't you?'

Casimir was silent.

'Yes. I see you do,' said Princess Christina. 'Well. I think I've made my point, so we'll leave it at that. Finish your coffee, Casimir. I'm sure we'll see each other again very soon.'

Casimir gulped down his coffee to the last bitter grains. Princess Christina opened a drawer and produced a small, gold object. 'Take this. If you need to see me at any time, it will make sure you are brought directly to me. And Casimir,' she added, 'I'm sure I needn't tell you that this conversation is not to be repeated to anyone. Especially not to your father.'

Casimir returned to the anteroom, the taste of Princess Christina's marzipan lingering on his tongue. In his hand was the token she had given him, a gold ring like a wedding band, with a pattern of roses around the rim. There was no crest or royal device or motto, nor was the ring especially valuable. It was anonymous and unremarkable. Casimir knew the princess was far too clever to have given him anything that would be traceable if it fell into the wrong hands.

He put the ring in his pocket. A footman was waiting for him with his own coat and shirt and when he had changed back into them he was shown out, this time via a route that afforded him a glimpse of the state apartments. The chandeliers in the great ballroom were being filled with wax candles for the queen's Christmas ball, and the voices of the servants echoed hollowly in the cavernous space; in another room, he saw musicians practising on strings, oboes and recorders. It was all glass and parquetry and red silk curtains, as grand and decadent as Casimir could possibly have hoped for, but he was too disturbed now by what had happened to pay it much attention.

He had told Princess Christina virtually everything she wanted to know. On the balance, he thought, it was hard to imagine how he could have escaped with doing anything else, but the difficulty now lay in guessing how she was going to use what he had told her. Nominally at least, the princess controlled the Queen's Guard. Casimir had never been able to understand how Ruth and her friends managed to reconcile this fact with the princess's supposedly liberal politics, but perhaps they knew things he did not. The myths were legion, and he had never worked out exactly how much control Christina wielded over the guard and how much its procurator, her future brother-in-law, wielded over her.

Despite its name, the Queen's Guard had nothing at all to do with the queen. In the past, it sometimes had. Queen Elsabetta's grandfather, King Frederik II, had been soft in the head; as he grew increasingly madder, his wife Sophia had been appointed Regent against the wishes of most of his council. On the advice of her brother, Nicholas of Osterdale, Queen Sophia had drawn from the Household Guard enough men with the right talent and disposition to create a separate and efficient spy network of her own. The Queen's Guard had quickly become a force to be reckoned with, and, on her death, Sophia had bequeathed it to her son's wife, Queen Elsabetta's mother, Elena. But Queen Elena's had been a less exceptional personality than her mother-in-law's, while her husband, Frederik III, had been interested in little else but amassing paintings and building palaces. A series of strong procurators, all drawn from Sophia's family, had been all it had taken for the Queen's Guard to slip from royal control; the Osterdales soon used it to take effective charge of the royal council, and were later strongly implicated in the downfall of Elena's successor, Astrid. By the time its command had descended to Astrid's daughter, Christina, it was a moot point as to whether it reported to anyone at all. The Queen's Guard—Sophie's Leeches in popular parlance—policed the city, controlled the press and monitored public opinion; it even had its own prison, the notorious Undercroft, into which people disappeared seemingly at random. Outside of Starberg, its powers were only slightly less despotic. While few people in Ostermark had any direct dealings with it, it was a rare man or woman who was not afraid to hear its name mentioned in conjunction with their own.

And now the queen was to marry the procurator, her cousin, the Margrave Greitz. Elsabetta, gentle, musical and politically obtuse, was more interested in her viols and recorder-players than in government; she was also reputedly in love with her cousin. That the match might not be wise had apparently not occurred to her. At least, that was what Ruth said, but plenty of other people were concerned enough for there to be widespread mutterings in the city. The Queen's Guard was powerful enough without its procurator becoming effectual King of Ostermark. As for Princess Christina, Casimir guessed it could only erode her already equivocal position further.

He arrived home to find Ruth's coach waiting—he supposed, inevitably—in the mews that ran along the back of Fish Lane. The kitchen window was open and there was a faint smell of woodsmoke from the chimney. As if on cue, when Casimir let himself into the yard, the back door opened and his father appeared. He had shed his red coat and waistcoat and wore his shirtsleeves rolled up over his elbows, the neck of his shirt unbuttoned despite the cold.

'Where the hell have you been?'

'I'm sorry, I didn't mean to—'

'Stop making excuses. I said, where the hell have you been?' Before Casimir had a chance to answer, Simeon grabbed him by the shoulder and shook him so hard he lost his balance and fell heavily on the cobblestones. A sharp pain shot through his knee and then Simeon dragged him to his feet again and dealt him a stinging slap across the face. Casimir yelled, partly from pain, but more from shock. Even allowing for the wintry weather, Simeon's hand against his bare flesh was icy cold.

His other hand twisted in Casimir's collar and he slapped him again, the way he had when Casimir was seven and had almost drowned swimming in the swift-running upper reaches of the Ling. Casimir struggled to free himself. Meanwhile, two other people had appeared in the doorway of the house. One was Ruth, which was not surprising, but the other was a tall, dark-haired man with a beard and a tatterdemalion aspect. He stepped forward out of the shadows, and his face was the mirror image of Casimir's own.

'Come on, Simeon,' the man said mildly. 'Don't you think you're overreacting a little? The boy's just stepped out for a moment. No harm done that I can see.'

For a split second, Simeon paused. He looked from Casimir to the newcomer, and then he let go Casimir's shoulder and jerked his head curtly towards the house. Casimir scuttled inside. As he passed Ruth in the doorway she pulled back her cloak, as if even the touch of his sleeve would somehow contaminate her.

Inside, the kitchen looked frowzy and untidy, dirty plates and cups on the table, and a scattering of unfamiliar possessions around the room. A grubby canvas pack sat steaming on the hearth and a bedroll stood propped in the corner. Casimir's eyes went straight to the stained military topcoat hanging over the edge of the table. Its brass buttons and epaulettes had long since been cut off, but Casimir recognised it immediately, for he had seen the same coat every winter for as long as he could remember. A moment later the coat's owner came into the kitchen. He had grown a little fatter and greyer in the twelve months since Casimir had seen him, and a few more lines had developed around his eyes, but otherwise he was the same: Casimir's uncle, Joachim Leibnitz, his mother's brother, who had been gunner's mate with his father and their friend for as long as he could remember.

'Hello, Cas,' he said. 'I see you haven't lost your talent for getting into trouble.'

Simeon came in behind him and shut the door. 'You've got some explaining to do,' he said shortly. 'I told you to stay inside. And you left without dousing the kitchen fire. It was still burning when we got back.'

'I'm sorry.' The fire was, Casimir thought, an adequate explanation for his father's anger, but he did not think it was the real one. 'I couldn't help it, I had to go out. Princess Christina sent for me to go to the palace.'

'Christina sent for *you*?' Ruth's words came out almost as a hiss of shock. Casimir felt piqued. Ruth's reaction, however, was completely overshadowed by Simeon's. He said nothing, but left the room abruptly. A moment later they heard his footsteps running up the stairs.

'What's up?' asked Joachim.

Ruth shrugged. She sat down at the kitchen table and dabbled a manicured fingertip in a puddle of coffee.

'I don't know what the problem is. He won't tell me, just that there's this man called Circastes who wants revenge on him. If you want to know more, perhaps you'd better ask Casimir.'

'Don't worry, I will.' The expression on Joachim's face left Casimir in no doubt that he knew exactly who Circastes was. A moment later the kitchen door opened and Simeon re-entered.

'I was right,' he said. 'There's a guardsman hiding in Petersen's house opposite. They're watching us.'

'You mean, we're not going to be able to get away?' blurted out Casimir. The words had scarcely left his mouth when he realised his mistake.

'What do you mean, get away?' said Ruth ominously. 'Where are you going?'

'Nowhere,' said Simeon. 'Nowhere at all.' He shot Casimir a savage look and stalked back out of the room.

Immediately Ruth shoved back her chair and hurried after him. The workroom door slammed shut. A moment later the sound of voices could be heard along the passage, softly at first, then raising swiftly in anger.

'Well,' said Joachim in conversational voice, 'I will say this. She's certainly nothing like your mother.'

'No,' said Casimir. 'She's not.'

He sat down at the kitchen table and buried his face in his hands. He was trembling. But even while he felt swamped by his own stupidity, Simeon's anger, and worst of all, the prospect of the Queen's Guard at their door on the very night they had planned to escape, a small warning beat like a pulse inside his brain. In the three hours since Simeon had left to go to the palace, something had happened. He did not yet know what it was, but the dynamics of their relationship had shifted, and he was sure it could bode no good.

Joachim moved his topcoat to the chair Ruth had just vacated and retrieved his pack from the hearthstone. His fingers ripped through the fastenings and it fell open on the table; he removed the top layer of clothing and started emptying it of letters, small books, pamphlets. He had not quite finished when the door creaked open and Ruth's face appeared.

'Casimir, my coachman has arrived. I need you to let me out.'

'You know where the key is.'

Ruth shook her head. Casimir sighed and pushed back his chair. He followed her along the passage. As they entered the shop, she turned and spoke to him in a low, swift voice.

'Casimir, I have to talk to you. I must know what's happening. Your father tried to resign his warrant for the wedding—'

'I don't know anything about it.'

'You *do* know.' She stared at him angrily. 'You're as bad as your father. Keep your secrets to yourself then. I don't expect you to tell me the truth. But whatever you do, don't let Simeon try to leave Starberg. The mood he's in today, he's capable of anything. I've never seen him like this.'

'Nor have I,' said Casimir. The confidence slipped out before he could help himself, and Ruth looked surprised.

'It's not you who's brought the guard here, it wasn't your fault,' she said unexpectedly. 'They'll have been watching you ever since Friday night. And the fact that they're doing that doesn't have to mean anything. I'll talk to Christina again and see what can be done. But Simeon must understand: if he tries to run, there'll be no helping him. He'll end up in the Undercroft and that will be the end of both of you.'

And you too, thought Casimir. He didn't say it, though, but simply nodded and went over to the counter. As he retrieved the key from its hook, Ruth's eye fell on the letter that Tycho had left earlier. Her lips pursed in apparent recognition of the handwriting.

'What's that?'

'Nothing.'

'Then you won't mind if I take it.'

She reached out a hand to the shelf where it was sitting, but Casimir was quicker. He took the letter and put it into his pocket. For a moment he met Ruth's eyes squarely. She did not drop her gaze, but she at least had the grace to blush.

'A word of warning, Casimir,' she said. 'My cousin is harmless, but unwise. He has been writing to many people lately, including myself. I know what's probably in that letter. My advice, for what it is worth, is to put it in the fire.'

Casimir put it back on the shelf.

'I'll see to it.'

'Do.'

Casimir watched her go out to her coach, picking her way through the puddles in her fur-lined cloak. The footman climbed down from the back to help her in, and the vehicle turned awkwardly in the narrow lane and drove away. Casimir waited until it had gone, then opened the door and went out into the street. Simeon had said the man who was watching them was in Petersen's house, opposite, but the windows were still boarded up and it looked deserted as it had since its owner had died three months before. It was possible, of course, that his father was mistaken, but Casimir did not think it likely. With a sense of sadness, he acknowledged that the game had moved beyond him and he no longer knew what Simeon was capable of or not.

After a while, he gave up and went back inside. On his way past the counter, he noticed that the shelf behind it was empty and that Tycho's letter was gone. There was, he thought, a faint—a very faint—odour of magic. But it was hard to be certain whether it was stale or fresh, or whether it was simply the scent of unexploded gunpowder, waiting to be set off.

CHAPTER FIVE

When Casimir came back into the kitchen he found Joachim sitting at the table, sorting through a stack of papers. The fire was burning and flickering and there was a familiar crackle of burning paper. As Casimir watched, his uncle tossed a sheaf of dog-eared pamphlets into the flames.

'Alas,' he said, 'the price of failure for a writer. If you don't sell, you burn.'

Casimir sat down. 'Where's Simeon?'

'Out. He left just a moment ago. Don't ask where he's gone, I couldn't tell you. He didn't volunteer the information and a man of my proclivities knows better than to ask.'

Joachim cut the twine on another bundle of papers and started sorting through them. They were the remains of his last year's stock, for he was, ostensibly at least, a travelling bookseller and printer's agent. Joachim delivered books, newspapers and catalogues to outlying districts, and made a specialty of items too scabrous and seditious to be available through ordinary channels. Every winter, around Christmas, his travels brought him back to Starberg, where Casimir and Simeon had made a habit of meeting up with him for winter lodgings. Except from queens, who could watch from the comfort of their heated palaces, there was not much call for firework displays in the dead of winter. While the Runcimans made stockpiles of fireworks, Joachim visited printers, stocked up on new titles, and delivered private letters whose contents were too sensitive to entrust to normal channels. Most of his time though, was spent renewing the network of information and contacts which was his real business. There was, as Joachim liked to tell Casimir, no money to speak of in books. He might have added, spying was much more profitable.

Casimir picked some woodcuts up from the table and started leafing through them. Their subject matter would have been enough to land both of them in the Undercroft if seen by the wrong eyes, but Casimir was too used to Joachim's activities to be really worried. Halfway through the pile his attention was arrested by a familiar face. The woodcut, crudely done on cheap stock, was captioned simply, *Invitation to a Royal Wedding*. It showed Queen Elsabetta, slightly smudged and literally falling out of her dress, lying on a sofa with her cousin, the Margrave Greitz. The procurator had his pants down, and the queen's arms were twined around his neck, but Casimir was more interested in a third figure, also female, which was shown creeping up behind them and reaching for the crown on the side table. A bubble was coming out of her mouth: *Sister, can I play, too?* With its long hair, round eyes and tiny coronet, it was unmistakably Princess Christina.

'That's sick,' he said, not altogether disapprovingly.

'Yes, it is, isn't it,' Joachim agreed. 'I'll have some new ones soon, if you're interested.' He took the picture from Casimir and divided the rest of the woodcuts carefully into two neat stacks. One, he tied up with twine and put back into his pack, along with several wax-sealed letters. The rest, including the questionable picture of the queen, he tossed into the fire.

'Better to play safe if the leeches are onto us,' he said. 'I'll get Simeon to pay me back in drinks when he's himself again. Ah, dear old Starberg! How I love it. There's nothing in Ostermark to quite match it for atmosphere. The cold, the stink, the Queen's Guard at your back every step you take: I sometimes wonder why I ever leave.' He leaned back in his chair and stretched. 'Now. You and I have some catching up to do. What's this I hear about Circastes?'

'It's nothing, really,' said Casimir awkwardly. 'I'm almost back to normal. It was more an accident than anything else.'

'An accident? I can see why the charming Ruth told me to talk to you,' said Joachim. 'Don't play games, Cas. You forget, I was there when this happened to your mother. Do you really think I'm going to stand back and watch it all happen again, just because you don't want to talk about it? I want you to go right back to the beginning. Take your time. And remember, if you don't tell me everything, I'll find out anyway.'

'Circastes attacked me in the park,' Casimir began reluctantly. Then he stopped. The enormity of what he had experienced, of what he was still experiencing, pressed so closely he did not know how to put his feelings into words. He blurted out, 'He got inside my head. It was horrible,' and as he spoke, the whole shuddering awfulness of Friday night came rushing back. The mist on the lake, the rain, the smell of the fallen leaves in the park, and Simeon walking towards him through the firework smoke with his firepot swinging at his side. And then the pull from the machine, the smell of the magic competing with the waft of gunpowder, and the numbing shock of the moment when his neck had snapped and for a few seconds he had died. Casimir began to shake. He had not thought he would be able to describe what had happened to anyone: not the fear, nor the panic, nor the sense of powerlessness and incredulity as his body had hit the ground. But now, after the two worst days of his life, the words came, almost tripping him up with the intensity of reliving the experience, and though he almost broke down completely when he came to the description of what had happened when he fell from the machine, he did not leave anything out. Joachim listened intently, not interrupting, but merely interposing the occasional question when he did not understand. But his face grew increasingly drawn as the account progressed, and at last, when Casimir had finished, he said,

'And Simeon? Has he said anything at all to you about this?'

Casimir shook his head. 'No. Hardly anything. He just told me who Circastes was and how to avoid him, and he didn't even want to do that. I think he only told me because he had to. But the worst of it is, he's been acting really strangely. One moment he's normal, the next he's biting my head off. And he's been using his magic for all sorts of things, like making lights and fetching letters. He's never done that before. It's like some sort of stopper's come out of a bottle and the magic just keeps spewing out.'

'Perhaps the bottle's had the stopper in it for too long.'

'But Simeon says magic is wrong.'

'No doubt. But that doesn't mean he doesn't use it when he has to,' said Joachim. 'Cas, you're not going to like this, but try and look at this from Simeon's point of view. He's been staving this crisis off since he was seventeen. Do you really think a man that desperate wouldn't use the one truly effective weapon he has at his disposal? I can assure you, he's not evaded Circastes all these years by putting on a uniform and hiding in the artillery train at the bum end of the Ostermark army, or by doing a flit to the next town every six months either. Of course he's used his magic. He wouldn't have survived five minutes if he hadn't.'

'I never realised,' said Casimir miserably.

'No reason why you should,' said Joachim. 'Simeon is secretive by nature, and he knows how to cover his tracks. I remember the first time I found out what he was. We were in the army and sharing a tent, and I surprised him one night putting wards on the canvas. Yet if I hadn't come back off guard duty at that particular moment, I would probably never have found out. Simeon reckons small spells that are continuous and don't require much energy can pass for years more or less unnoticed. And let's face it, Cas, your work is full of funny smells. This shop stinks. A little whiff of something extra wouldn't make much of an impression.'

'It's not *that* bad,' objected Casimir.

'Isn't it? The fact is, you're so close to it, you're past noticing. And for that matter, I've often had my doubts about some of Simeon's fireworks. Think of those girandoles that levitate off their poles, and the way his set pieces move as if they're almost alive. Then there's the colours no other firework maker can get, the blues and greens—'

'That's not magic, that's chemicals,' said Casimir defensively. 'Barium for green, zinc for blue. Anyone could do it if they knew the mix.'

'I'll bow to your professional opinion,' said Joachim, 'but in any case we're straying from the subject. What I'm trying to tell you is this: whatever Simeon may say, he has made his choice and he cannot walk away from it. The magic is part of him. It's in his blood and his bones by his own resolution and he is fooling himself if he says he can live without it.'

Casimir took this in. 'Joachim. Can I ask you something?'

'Of course.'

'Do you ever see my mother?'

'Now, there's an interesting question,' said Joachim. 'What makes you ask after her all of a sudden?'

'Nothing. Just curious, I suppose.'

'She's been gone eight years and you've never been curious before. Never wondered where she was, what she was doing? Never thought to ask me how she was getting along?'

Something in his tone stung Casimir's already lacerated nerves. 'Of course I wondered about her. She's my mother. But Simeon would never have let me ask you, so there wasn't any point. Anyway, did she ever ask about me?'

'No. Never,' said Joachim, flatly, and he went on, with a glance at Casimir's shocked expression, 'believe that, Cas, with all your heart. I could tell you a lot of things about your mother if I wanted to, and any or all of them could be true. But I am never going to tell you where she is. Simeon has ways and means at his disposal. If I told you, he'd winkle it out of you in an instant.'

'He could winkle it out of you, too.'

'He could,' Joachim agreed. 'But I promise you, he won't.'

He stood up, picked up his topcoat, and put it on over his leather waistcoat. Then he pulled a battered hat down over his eyes and slung his pack over his shoulder.

'I have to go out. I've got people to see and messages to deliver. We'll talk some more when I come back. If you could go out to the front and create some sort of diversion, it'd help.'

'All right.' Casimir pushed back his chair. At the passage doorway, he paused and looked back over his shoulder. 'Where exactly are you going?'

'Ah,' said Joachim reprovingly. 'That would be telling.'

Casimir fetched a rag and a bucket of water from the workshop and took them out into the street. For ten minutes or so he made a play of cleaning the shop windows, which were in truth extremely dirty. He felt jumpy. While Joachim was prone to embellishment in the interests of a good story, he knew that he never dramatised risk. If he wanted a diversion while he got away, the chances that he needed one were very good.

Across the street was Petersen's place, where Simeon had claimed someone was watching. It looked much as it had for the last few months, ever since its owner had died and the fever commissioners had boarded it up. Casimir went out into the middle of the street to empty his bucket into the gutter and get a better look, and a figure in the familiar black and scarlet uniform came out of another building along the street. It could easily have been a coincidence, but Casimir knew it wasn't. The leeches were trying to frighten him; they wanted him to know he was being watched. Casimir went back inside to eat a belated, solitary lunch and sew Princess Christina's gold ring into his pillow for safekeeping. Then, since he had nothing better to do, he went into the workroom.

Ordinarily, there would have been lots to occupy him. For months, Elsabetta's wedding had kept them working every daylight hour: now, with no guarantee they would even be staying in Starberg, and his hands still in bandages, it was hard for Casimir to know what to do. In the end, he got out a ball of twine and sat winding it around the paper cases of the firework shells. It was a dull and painstaking job and one he normally skived off doing, but this afternoon he found the patient weaving and knotting suited his agitated mood. Each shell was a cylinder, made by winding and gluing strips of stiff brown paper around a wooden form. The cylinder contained circular patterns of crackers, running rockets and stars, tamped down and interspersed with black powder; at the bottom was the priming chamber, which was filled with gunpowder, and a touch-hole through which protruded the fuse. Until they had settled in Starberg and established the shop, Casimir's experience of shells had been limited. He and Simeon only owned the one small mortar in their window and it was generally more practical for travelling pyrobolists to use rockets. But rockets needed large amounts of gunpowder to carry them into the sky, meaning the space inside for stars and crackers was limited; shells were more spectacular, and could even be designed to burst in a series of different coloured explosions. For the queen's wedding, Simeon had negotiated with the Master of the Ordnance for the use of as many military mortars as they needed; he had taught Casimir how to calculate the launching charge and the size of the shell in relation to the calibre of the mortar, and how to make salutes by filling the shell with cut reeds packed with gunpowder. And in passing, he had touched on their military applications, telling him how to replace the harmless stars with nails and shrapnel that would tear a man's head off. This afternoon it occurred to Casimir for the first time that, in doing this, Simeon might have had an ulterior motive. If they left Starberg without their tools, powder and equipment, they could no longer make fireworks themselves; nor could they expect to find work with other pyrobolists, who mostly employed members of their own families. But men who could mix black powder and operate cannon were valuable commodities in any army, and at fourteen, especially with his skills, Casimir was more than old enough to enlist, too.

Casimir put down his ball of twine. The possibility that Simeon had been considering re-enlisting terrified him. He had no dreams of heroism, no hopes of glory and the prospect of fighting for his living made his stomach curdle. Intellectually, Casimir had always known that Simeon had killed people. All soldiers had to, at random and without compunction, but most of the time he had conveniently managed not to think about it. Artillerymen were the outcasts in any army. Filthy, notoriously foul-mouthed, shoved to the back of the baggage train where their black work posed less of a threat to their fellow soldiers, they were feared and shunned by ally and enemy alike. Helplessly, Casimir looked around the firework workshop, at the pots of gum arabic, the basket of reeds for the salutes, the apothecary's scales, driving bench and all the arcane tools of his trade. There were wooden mallets and sharp knives for cutting paper, neat pottery containers labelled *Camphire*, *Quickmatch*, *Flowers of Benjamin*; pots of gaily-coloured paint and glistening paper stars, jars of frankincense and civet for Simeon's special perfumed water globes. A stack of tiny red rocket caps drooped on the bench, like hats for miniature Chinese. As he looked at all these things it occurred to Casimir that within these walls he had made the firework boy and learned the final mysteries of the craft he had been trained up in since childhood, and that despite Ruth and Simeon and even Circastes, he did not want to leave what he had learned behind. The power to make people laugh and shout out loud with joy and excitement, painstakingly gained over so many years in peaceful towns and villages, at fairs and festivals, was the only magic he wanted to wield. And whatever happened to him now, he knew he did not want to use it to kill people.

His equanimity had gone and a depression settled slowly over him in its place. For a while Casimir worked on, but it was hard to shake off the feeling that he was wasting his time. In the end the daylight went and he found himself sitting in the dark. Casimir put away his tools and went back to the kitchen. He had put out the fire when Joachim left and had to fumble in the dark for the tinderbox; when he found it, the dampness in the air affected the tinder and it refused to glow. As Casimir knelt to fish some half-burned paper out of the fireplace, yet another anomaly occurred to him: that Simeon, so insistent that their unattended fires always be doused, could nevertheless always get one going whenever he wanted in a matter of seconds. The thought of his father casually using magic to light their fires made Casimir irrationally angry. He suddenly wanted to lash out and defy him, to call Simeon a hypocrite and tell him what he thought of his secrecy. But Simeon was not there. And instead, as if from nowhere, a thought insinuated itself into his head like a snake winding its way out of a wicker basket: that magic was not the only way to light a fire.

Casimir put his hand into his pocket and closed his fingers over a piece of quickmatch which he had trimmed off one of the shells earlier in the afternoon. It would burn brighter and faster than any tinder, and a spark from the flint and steel, a handful of black powder judiciously placed among the kindling would soon get a fire going. The irresponsibility of the idea went against every tenet of Casimir's training and every grain of common sense as well. Simeon would be furious, and that thought filled him with a twisted delight. Before Casimir knew what he was doing he was walking out of the kitchen and down the darkened passageway to the workroom.

There was gunpowder in barrels just inside the workroom door. It did not travel or store well, so Simeon mixed it himself regularly in the powder cellar under the shop, and brought it up as it was needed. Gently, Casimir prised the lid off the first barrel. It contained a slow composition used in rockets and had a high proportion of charcoal that would suit his purposes well. He selected a measure and dipped it into the gritty, pungent mixture.

It was a soft pop which alerted him, a sound like a thumb being pulled out of a mouth. Showering gunpowder, he spun around just in time to see the air glimmer and a huge shell disappear from the workbench. Casimir took an involuntary step forward and his feet crunched on powder. Another shell disappeared, and another, and another. Then, to his right, the driving bench suddenly rattled into phosphorescent life, the paper rocket cases shaking down from their box into upright positions. Black powder flowed down into them from the reservoirs above and the wooden mallet Simeon used to tamp it down into the rockets started lifting and falling, as though held by an invisible hand.

A smell gathered in the workroom and rolled towards Casimir like a wave. On the workbench the rocket caps flew, to and fro, fastening themselves to the finished cases, which then rolled off into a basket that rocked merrily on the flagstones; the twine unrolled and coiled around the unfinished shells which shimmered and disappeared in on themselves, giving the impression of an implosion. Suddenly there was a loud bang: the lids had flown off the barrels of fine birch charcoal, saltpetre and sulphur which Simeon used to mix their powder. Their contents poured up and out in three great arcs that twined together, like a three-stranded plait that swirled blackly and disappeared into nothingness.

All this time, Casimir stood watching the fireworks making themselves, the black powder mixing and eddying away. The temperature in the room dropped, like the bitter cold before a storm, and the smell of magic gathered like a mist. Then the windows rattled and the floor shook and the paper stars and the firework cases and all the trumpery tackle of his trade suddenly lifted off the shelves. They whirled around him in a blinding, stinging storm until Casimir could stand no more, but turned and ran in terror from the room.

CHAPTER SIX

T he whole ground floor was awash with the smell of magic.

Casimir ran up the stairs two at a time. He did not stop until he had reached his attic, bolted the door and flung open the one low window as wide as it would go. Below him, Fish Lane had settled down for the evening. There were lights in the windows of some of the houses. No one, not even the Queen's Guard, seemed to have noticed anything unusual except him.

Casimir pulled away from the window and sat down with a thump. He buried his face in his hands and pinched his nose in a desperate attempt to quell his rising hysteria. Until this moment, it had never occurred to him to doubt his sanity. What had happened in the park had been an isolated incident, a freak which he had struggled to persuade himself would not happen again. But now there could be no doubt. Circastes had not gone away: he was out there, like a cat waiting for a mouse at a crack in the wainscot. Casimir wondered whether he was going mad, whether Circastes had forced his way into his head like a thief intent on robbing him of his equanimity. In the silence of his attic he could not even be sure whether the whole thing had been a grand delusion. Then he heard a noise on the roof above him and looked up fearfully.

The slates creaked and there was a scraping, sliding sound as if someone was coming down the pitched section at the back of the house. For a moment Casimir sat listening, and then his paralysis broke and he jumped and ran for the door. He wrenched the bolt from its fastener and flung it open; at that very moment the skylight opened above the landing and a dark figure jumped down like a thunderbolt in front of him.

Casimir screamed. He flung himself sideways and the intruder grabbed him by the scruff of the neck and shook him. When he struck out with his fist the man grunted, but did not let go; there was a moment's scuffle in which both of them flailed around and then, 'Be still, Cas!' a voice said fiercely. 'You fool! it's only me.' Casimir's last kick connected and the man suddenly let go and he fell onto the floor.

His uncle's face loomed over him, silhouetted by the faint gleam from the skylight. Casimir sat up.

'What are you doing, creeping around like that?' he said indignantly. 'I thought you were Circastes, breaking in.'

'Considering what I've been doing,' said Joachim, 'and the fact that the leeches are watching this building, you surely don't think I'd be stupid enough to come in through the door?' He reached up a long arm and closed the skylight with a snap. 'Anyway, why would a magician come sneaking in through a skylight? I think he could manage a flashier entrance, don't you?'

Casimir scrambled to his feet. 'Circastes has been here already. There was something in the workroom, it all went crazy. All the fireworks started making themselves. I ran away and then I heard someone on the roof. Of course I thought you were him. Who else could it have been?'

'All sorts of people,' said Joachim. 'Me. Or even Simeon for that matter. Besides, how do you know it was Circastes in the workroom? There are two magicians in Starberg at the moment that I know of. If someone's practising magic in this house, it's just as likely to have been your father.' He started down the stairs, his boots echoing loudly in the stairwell. 'Come on. If you're right, we're not going to avoid trouble by hiding in the attic.'

He disappeared around the bend in the staircase and Casimir heard him descending, his footsteps getting gradually fainter. Casimir's hands were trembling. He felt almost too frightened to follow, but then he heard his uncle's voice calling up reassuringly from the ground floor, and somehow he managed to put his legs into motion. Tread by tread, he felt his way down the darkened stairs. At the bottom he thought he caught a lingering whiff of the magic smell, but that was all.

Joachim was standing inside the workroom, regarding the destruction. 'Well,' he said. 'It's a bit of a mess, I'll agree. If Simeon's not responsible, I wouldn't like to be here when he finds out.'

Casimir sidled up behind him. The window was open and rain had blown inside. A stack of rocket caps had fallen in a puddle on the work bench. There were sodden paper stars and a quantity of wet powder on the floor.

'I left the window shut.' Casimir went over and checked it. The catch seemed unbroken. Several dozen unfinished shells still sat on the workbench, but it was hard to tell how many of the finished ones were missing. The rocket basket beside the driving bench was empty.

'Are you sure you weren't dreaming?' said Joachim, cynically. Casimir shot him a filthy look, and he went on, 'Don't worry. I don't necessarily disbelieve you. But it's always a possibility and the question has to be asked.'

'I wasn't dreaming,' said Casimir flatly.

'In that case, there's nothing we can do until Simeon comes back. Let's close up and have a drink.'

Casimir shut the window and they crunched back through the wet gunpowder to the door. In the kitchen they got the fire going and lit the candles. The room at once felt cheerier and Casimir started to relax a little. Joachim rummaged inside his pack and produced a leather bottle.

'Here. That'll put some fire in you. Is there anything to eat?'

'Cold pie. Some bread. There's beer in the keg.' While Joachim busied himself drawing ale and hacking up the pie, Casimir unstoppered the bottle and drank from it deeply. The spirit burned his throat, but he followed his first swig with a second and felt better when his legs went weak beneath him. Joachim handed him a plateful of food and a knife. He hung his topcoat on the back of the door and began removing his sodden clothing.

'You don't have to drink it all,' he remarked. 'Leave some for your old uncle: it's cold outside.' His fingers ripped through the buttons on his leather waistcoat and he draped a long tattered scarf over the back of a kitchen chair. Casimir handed back the bottle. It was almost empty and he knew in a minute he was going to be horribly drunk.

'Joachim,' he said, 'do you think I could be going mad?'

'That depends on how you define madness,' said Joachim. 'You've always seemed sane enough to me and I doubt you're headed for the asylum. On the other hand, if you are worried whether someone is magically deluding you, then I'm afraid I honestly don't know. Why?'

'I thought Circastes had got into my head again. Then I thought—I thought for a moment, maybe it was me. That I'd cracked. That something had come out of me that I didn't know was there. But it's not like that, is it?' Casimir pleaded. 'Just because Simeon is—it doesn't mean that I am, does it?'

'Do you mean, a magician?' Casimir nodded, and Joachim shook his head. 'It doesn't work like that, Cas. Magic is a skill, an ability you acquire. You could certainly choose to become a magician, if you wanted to. But it isn't something you're born with, like red hair or flat feet.'

'But a magician can send you mad, can't he?' The pent-up fear was suddenly released by the emotion and the alcohol. 'It was what happened to my mother, wasn't it? Wasn't it?'

Joachim looked at him, not unkindly. 'Don't you remember?'

Casimir shrugged and stared at the table. A small child's muddled memories came back to him. He remembered Simeon fetching him in the middle of the night, his hair and clothes pungent with the smell of magic. He remembered a journey through the darkness in a military carrier's cart, nights under canvas, nights in the open, nights in dirty lodgings, sleeping in Simeon's arms. But Jessica's departure he could not remember at all. His mother had simply vanished, and Simeon had never even told him why she had gone.

'They weren't happy together,' said Joachim softly. 'Simeon was always difficult and she was just—wild, I suppose. When he spouted his crazy ideas, talked about free will and the destruction of oppressive power structures, she just laughed at him. And then she went out and did what she damn well liked. It was what had attracted him to her in the first place, but it didn't make them a compatible couple.'

'What happened?' said Casimir.

'Circastes found them,' said Joachim. 'Simeon had grown careless. He'd stayed in the same place for too long, for one thing, and then, he'd started circulating his ideas in writing. That was foolish. It drew attention to him, and since his theories were mostly a reaction to what he'd learned when he was a magician, it didn't take much for Circastes to make the connection. You see, Casimir, magic is all about control. Control of inanimate objects, control of your immediate environment, but chiefly, control over other people. Simeon believes the type of magic he was taught dehumanises the victim by taking away their right to self-determination. That's why he has made such a fetish of free will in his politics. He's trying to atone for what he did and for the knowledge and skills he wishes he didn't have. And of course, Circastes understood exactly where all this was coming from.

'We were in Osterfall at the time; Simeon was working there as a powder monkey in one of the silver mines. Circastes found your mother alone at home. She invited him in without realising who he was and he got into her head, made her try to kill Simeon with a carving knife. I was there, I saw her do it. Simeon had to use magic to snap the hold Circastes had over her. And it broke her utterly. That's why Simeon's so frightened now. He's afraid that what he did to your mother he will end up doing to you.' Joachim paused. 'Your mother's not mad, Cas. She was too strong-willed to do anything but survive. But she became a different person in the process. The girl your father fell in love with is gone.'

'I'm afraid,' said Casimir simply. 'Sooner or later, Circastes is going to come. I don't know why he hasn't already. I don't know what Simeon's planning, I don't even know what he's thinking. I wanted to run away this evening, only I had nowhere to go to.'

'Running away won't solve anything,' said Joachim. 'Simeon's first instinct, to stay here, was right. I would like it better if he hadn't gone storming off, but I think the best thing we can do now is wait for him to come back. If he doesn't, we'll obviously have to rethink our options. But in that case I think we'll almost certainly have heard from Circastes first.'

※

Casimir had fully expected Simeon to return some time during the evening. But by ten o'clock, there was still no sign of him, and the combination of strong liquor, beer and mental exhaustion overcame his intention of sitting up. He went to bed, leaving Joachim reading in the kitchen, and slept so soundly that an army of magicians might have come over the roof without his noticing. When he woke the next morning, it was to the sound of church bells ringing discordantly across the city. Casimir lay in bed for a few minutes listening to them. It was a Monday, and at first he could not work out why they were ringing. Then, belatedly, he realised it was Christmas Eve. With all the disturbance over Circastes, he had completely forgotten the date.

Downstairs, he heard the shop door tinkle. The sound, and the fact that it was a working day—perhaps the busiest working day in their entire year—forced Casimir to roll out of bed and look for his clothes. He pulled them on, noted there were three extra hairs on his chin—soon, he thought optimistically, there would be so many he'd have to stop counting—and went downstairs. The shop was open and he could hear voices and people moving around inside. It seemed to be business as usual, and he felt a surge of optimism. But when he opened the door, instead of Simeon's familiar figure behind the counter, he found to his disappointment it was Joachim, a string of crackers around his neck and a catherine wheel pinned to his lapel.

'Sore head?' asked his uncle maliciously. The shop was full of customers and he was evidently doing a roaring trade. Casimir shrugged. His head was aching, but he'd had worse hangovers, and he knew he'd get no sympathy if he admitted it. Simeon was nowhere to be seen and it was clear he had not come back. A wave of depression washed over Casimir and he sat down on an empty powder barrel.

A man with an armful of fireworks handed his uncle a five crown piece. It seemed so little for all he was buying Casimir could not help but be distracted.

'Are you sure you've added that up right?'

Joachim shot him a meaningful glance. 'You've forgotten, nephew: it's our Christmas sale. I put the sign out first thing this morning. Half price on all fireworks, as long as I don't have to wrap them up. We've been very busy. I think the word must be spreading.'

'What?' Casimir looked around, saw how much was being purchased, and did some rapid mental arithmetic. He got up and hissed in his uncle's ear. 'What are you doing? That's our best stock you're selling. Those prices won't even pay for the gunpowder. When Simeon finds out, he'll kill you.'

'Wait a moment.' Joachim took some money from another customer, watched him leave, then pulled Casimir to one side, out of earshot of the other people in the shop. He whispered, 'Listen to me. Use your brains. You and Simeon are in deep trouble. If you have to run, the fireworks are worth nothing to you; you need cash, not catherine wheels and rockets. And you've got another problem you don't know about, yet, a big problem. About half an hour ago a man came here from the Ordnance Office. He says you have fifty-seven small calibre shell mortars on loan and he wants to check them. My guess is, he's been sent by the Queen's Guard. Somebody's tipped him off about what happened on Friday night.'

Casimir felt his stomach turn inside out. 'What did you tell him?'

'I said I was only an employee and I didn't know anything about it. He was displeased. He said he would come back and he's not going to be put off. This has been planned, Cas. He has written authorities, an inventory, and I wouldn't mind betting, a warrant for Simeon's arrest as well.'

'The mortars are all at Ruth's place,' said Casimir, dismayed. 'Simeon borrowed them for the display on Friday, we have them on loan until the wedding. He told Ruth's servants to put them away in the stables.'

'If that's the case you'd better go and look at them. Check them, count them, make sure they're all in working order. Because the fellow was talking about taking them back and if there's anything amiss, I'll lay you an odds-on bet it'll be used as an excuse to take you and Simeon into custody.'

A woman with a gaggle of children came trailing up to the counter. Casimir backed off and slipped away in a state of considerable upheaval. Joachim was right: he had to go to Ruth's immediately. Unlike Simeon, he did not have a permanent passport for the River Court and Palace Precincts, but he still had his expired pass from Friday. Casimir took out his pocket knife, which he mostly used for cutting fuses, and neatly trimmed off the stamp the sentry had put on the bottom of the document. Then he found a pen and altered Friday's date, 21 December, by changing the figure one into a skinny four. It was not a very professional job, but he hoped the guards would not look too closely. On Christmas Eve, with any luck, they would have other things on their minds.

It was only a ten-minute walk to the River Court, down wide, paved streets through the better part of town. The old king, Christina and Elsabetta's father, had cleared the inner city in the early part of his reign, demolishing the slums and banishing their inhabitants to the other side of the river. Only a few old buildings had been allowed to remain, notably the university, the cathedral and the Undercroft. Casimir generally preferred not to pass its ugly bulk unless he had to, but today, he was in a hurry. The Undercroft was the headquarters of the Queen's Guard, a squat, stone building originally built as a grain store. It had few windows and massive walls that had been extended, strengthened and reinforced several times. Only one door was visible, but there were reputedly many hidden ones, mostly underground and linked into a legendary network of tunnels that criss-crossed the city. Casimir did not know whether to believe in these tunnels, but many people did. According to popular legend, Queen

Sophia's brother, Nicholas, the first procurator, had been lured into one and murdered by angry partisans of a rival faction. The Queen's Guard had risen in bloody revolt; there had been riots in the streets and for days the Ling had been filled with the corpses of those accused of supporting the murderers. Queen Sophia had let them do it, then appointed her younger brother Henry as procurator in Nicholas's place. The Queen's Guard had emerged from the disaster stronger than ever. Somehow or other, it always did.

Casimir walked past the Undercroft on the other side of the street, and was not sorry when it disappeared behind him. He walked for a way along the river, taking a route through the Christmas markets and getting caught up in the throngs of well-dressed shoppers out to buy presents and the Christmas goose. Upmarket street stalls sold armfuls of greenery, hot potatoes, and nativity scenes in which the faces of the magi seemed to bear a disturbing resemblance to Circastes. This time last year he had been there himself, selling rockets off the back of a barrow. At last he reached the River Court with its black and yellow flags. A small crowd was gathered at the sentry box, and was being held back by two or three Household Guardsmen.

'The queen's going to the cathedral to listen to some new piece of music,' explained a woman when Casimir asked what was happening. 'They won't let us through until her coach has passed by.'

The crowd muttered and shuffled. A few people strained to see what was going on and one woman climbed upon her husband's shoulders and sighted over the iron railings. At last there was a flurry of activity. A gate opened and two coaches drawn by bay horses and flanked by an impressive collection of outriders pulled out onto the carriageway and drove away.

As the first coach passed, Casimir had a glancing view of a lace-edged hood at the window and underneath it a pale, female face with a long straight nose. That was all: his first and probably only glimpse of the woman whose forthcoming wedding had occupied almost all of his working life over the last six months, the woman for whom he had made the firework boy, and who had indirectly been the cause of his present dilemma. Queen Elsabetta was not nearly as pretty as her half-sister, Christina, but Casimir supposed she didn't have to be. The queen hadn't spent most of her life in exile because of a disgraced mother, and she hadn't needed to fight for her position at court. Elsabetta was neither glamorous nor beautiful; her artistic interests were too highbrow to appeal to her ordinary subjects, and her rule was ineffectual. She was, in short, a splendid nonentity. If the queen died tomorrow, Casimir guessed, it would cause a stir, but probably nobody except the royal musicians would be bothered to see her go.

The queen having left, the knot of people in front of him started moving towards the sentry box. Casimir showed his pass to the guard and, to his relief, was waved perfunctorily through. His arrival at the treasurer's stables was met with similar indifference. One of the stablehands fetched him the storeroom key from the undergroom, and pointed him in the direction of some stairs.

'Do you want a lantern?'

'Thanks.'

Casimir went down the stairs into a sort of well. At the bottom some logs, sacks and a shovel were piled in the corner beside a door and when Casimir turned the key in the lock it opened onto what looked like a cellar. He stepped inside and waited for his eyes to grow accustomed to the dimness. Sure enough, the mortars stood in front of him in mute rows like so many open mouths; behind them were stacks of fireworks, brought over from the shop during the last few weeks for storage. The room stank and with a sinking feeling Casimir realised it was from damp. The palace and all the surrounding buildings were built on fill. Nothing stood between them and the Ling except the River Court. After the last few days of almost constant rain, the river levels must have risen.

Casimir wiped a hand over the nearest mortar. His fingers came away smeared with a rusty film; it looked as if they had been put away wet after Friday's display and he guessed they would all need cleaning and greasing. Casimir counted them and was relieved to find none were missing; he turned to explore the rest of the cellar and shone his light over the old lumber and disused wine racks which lined the walls. The floor sloped down towards the river and was obviously damp. The more he saw, the more Casimir realised the recent rain had turned this cellar into the worst possible place to store fireworks. Even if the damp did not get into the well-caulked barrels full of rockets, the set pieces were wrapped only in canvas that would not be proof against the moisture in the air.

Simeon was normally meticulous about such things. The fact that he had neither checked, nor realised what was happening here, was an ominous indicator of his state of mind. At the lowest point of the room was a wooden door, its timbers warped and twisted. Casimir gave it a push, but it was locked and the wood was still good enough to hold. He knelt and tried to peer underneath it. Though it was too dark to see he caught a draught, and a pungent whiff of river. Whatever cellar or space was on the other side must stretch under the River Court in front of the palace and go right down to the water's edge below.

There was nothing else he could do there. Casimir turned and went back to the stairs. On the way out, he picked up a waxed roll of catherine wheels. When he reached the safety of the carriageway he extracted one from the packet and tried to light it. As he had expected, it was blind as a beggar on the cathedral steps. It probably didn't matter, since by the time of the wedding there was no saying where they might be, but the sheer waste irritated Casimir all the same. He wondered briefly what Simeon would say when he came back, and then suddenly it occurred to him that, of all the places in Starberg where his father might have spent the night, Ruth's house was the most likely. Casimir put away the lantern, kicked the blind firework into the gutter, and headed across the tunnel to the treasurer's residence.

As it turned out, Ruth was entertaining friends.

The treasurer's door was opened by a girl called Lilias, whom Casimir knew quite well. In the early days of his father's relationship with Ruth, before they opened the shop in Fish Lane, he had spent a lot of time hanging about the treasurer's kitchen. Lilias worked there as a kitchen maid. She was friendly and funny and disposed to chat, and Casimir had quickly grown to like her. If she hadn't been so fat he might even have fancied her, but things had never advanced that far. Later, when he'd heard she was seeing one of the stablehands, he'd been glad of this fact, and further along, when she'd dumped the stablehand for a junior footman, he'd congratulated himself on his escape. It was therefore extremely disconcerting that Lilias was so pleased to see him, and even more alarming that she insisted on pretending he had come to see her.

'Casimir! You poor thing. We heard all about the accident. I'm so relieved you're all right. Thank you so much for coming to tell me.'

'It was nothing—'

'And your poor hands, just look at them. It must have been terrible.' To Casimir's alarm, she immediately seized one of the poor hands in her own and started fondling it. Selfconsciously, he pulled it back and half wished he'd had the foresight to remove the bandages.

'They're almost better. Is Ruth home? The margravine, I mean.' He had been going to ask if Simeon had stayed the night but decided it might not be tactful. Lilias smiled and he noticed she had dimples. And nice eyes, green ones. . .

'She's upstairs. With some friends. Do you want someone to show you up?'

'No. No. Just tell me where it is and I'll find it.' Relief flooded through him as she rattled off some instructions, he had been afraid she would offer to take him up herself. But of course, she was kitchen staff and would not be allowed upstairs. Briefly, Casimir wondered whether Lilias was still involved with the footman. She had always been a terrible flirt, but all the same, it would be nice to know.

'I'll talk to you later,' he said on impulse, and she smiled again and went back into the kitchen. Casimir was smitten by a pang of guilt. Before there could be a next time he would probably no longer be in Starberg.

As at the palace, the treasurer's servants had their own corridors for moving about the house, with doors hidden in walls so they could appear and disappear when summoned or dismissed. Ruth's sitting room, Lilias had said, was off the second passage on the first floor, a particularly dark and narrow tunnel which made Casimir feel like a rat trapped in the wainscot. He found the door with difficulty, rapped, and listened at the jamb. A male voice called out in reply, and this stroke of luck—for he could not conceive of Ruth's companion being anyone other than Simeon—sent caution and commonsense flying to the winds. Casimir turned the handle and opened the door.

He realised his mistake immediately, but by then it was too late. Neither Ruth nor Simeon was in sight. It was not even a sitting room. Instead, a man in his late fifties was sitting alone at a small table, the remains of a splendid breakfast set before him. Casimir knew immediately who he was. He had seen Ruth's father once or twice from a distance, though he had never spoken to him; he knew, too, that Simeon had once been introduced and that, following a violent argument, the two men now avoided each other. 'He hates me,' Simeon had said. 'And he's got a vicious temper. If he could bar me from his house, he would. But he knows Ruth will complain to Christina, and even he acknowledges Christina is someone it pays not to annoy.' Now, as the treasurer put down his cup of chocolate, Casimir realised dismally that, in his case, Christina's influence was going to be no protection at all.

'What are you doing here?' the treasurer asked. 'You're Runciman's son, aren't you? I thought I recognised you. Where's—?' The expression that came out of his mouth was so foul and calculated that it was a few moments before Casimir realised he was actually referring to Simeon. He felt the colour drain out of his face. Hopefully, he lifted his packet of damp catherine wheels.

'I don't know where Simeon is. I've brought some fireworks. He asked me to meet him here.'

'Then he is guilty of an impertinence. This house is not a rendezvous. You have no right to come into it without my permission and nor does he. What do you think you're doing?'

'Nothing. I told you. Simeon wanted me to deliver some fireworks. There's a lot more in storage, under the stables, I've just been checking them.' Casimir knew he was babbling, but he could see the carefully controlled anger building up in the treasurer's expression. He was metering it out, like a length of slow match, and any moment he would reach the flashpoint. Then, unexpectedly, a door opened across the room and Ruth appeared.

Her father turned in his chair. Casimir looked from one to the other of them. In that instant he saw the focus of the man's anger shift, knew that Ruth had seen it too. She bowed to her father and said, 'Casimir, you've come to the wrong room. Please go into my sitting room across the passage and let my father finish his breakfast.' She held the door open and her eyes met his. 'Now, please.'

The dozen steps past the breakfast table were among the most difficult Casimir had ever taken. It was as if somebody had suddenly opened a window for him onto Ruth's life and a blast of rancid air had come streaming out. He did not know which of them he wanted to get away from the most. As he went into the passageway he heard Ruth say, 'Father, please. He's only a boy, for God's sake, he doesn't mean any harm,' and then the door closed, the slow match reached the powder keg, and the explosion went off in the room behind him.

Casimir stood in the corridor. Never before had he had reason to feel grateful to Ruth. He could almost feel sorry for her, for he had never heard invective uttered with the finesse and fluency with which her father now delivered it. Casimir was accustomed to the casual obscenities of fairgrounds and street markets, where foul language was normal and meant nothing, but this was something different, for it was done with deliberation and, he suspected, enjoyment. It was horribly compelling, and for a few moments he listened, not from pleasure at Ruth's suffering, but out of a sick necessity, as the treasurer turned his fury on his daughter, calling her every vile name imaginable, cutting her protests into tiny shreds, her remonstrations gradually becoming more and more feeble until she was virtually silent, and the only voice that was audible was her father's. Casimir moved away. Across the passage, Ruth's sitting room door was standing open, and, obeying her instructions for the first time in his life, he let himself inside and shut the door.

In his imagination, Casimir had always thought of Ruth living in the utmost luxury. That impression, based on ignorance and prejudice, was scarcely supported by the small, shabby room in which he now found himself. A little fat dog with a fluffy coat looked up from a battered settle as Casimir entered, then closed its eyes and dropped its head again; there was a small low desk under the window, a coal fire and an empty coffee cup on the side table. But most of all, there were books, lots of books. They burst out of bookcases, sprawled in piles on the carpet, and lay promiscuously jumbled on every available flat surface. Casimir looked at some of the titles, but could not work out any logic to their owner's reading tastes: there were books on politics, history and in foreign languages, plenty of poetry and fiction. Ruth seemed to read anything and everything she could lay her hands on, and for almost the first time Casimir was reluctantly obliged to admit a point of commonality between her and his father. If it ever came to a choice between buying a meal and a book, Casimir knew Simeon would choose the book every time.

On the desk was a letter in his father's beautiful, sloping black writing. An endearment, startlingly out of character, leaped off the page and sent a blush burning in Casimir's cheeks; he hastily turned the letter over and then, hit by an impulse so strong and automatic he could not resist it, he folded it up and tucked it into the pocket of his leather overcoat. A moment later the door opened and Ruth came into the room. Her face was pink and upset, and Casimir could not be certain whether or not she was about to cry. He desperately hoped she was not, but whatever her father had said, she was apparently equal to it, for she merely sat down on the settle and heaved a deep breath. The dog climbed, whining, onto her lap and she stroked it absently. Then, to Casimir's surprise, she said,

'All right, Casimir, sit down.'

Casimir was stunned. 'Don't you want me to leave?'

His response seemed to return Ruth to something resembling her normal self. 'Of course I don't want you to leave,' she snapped. 'Would I have asked you to sit down if I did? You've got some explaining to do, Casimir Runciman. What are you here for? And don't try and fob me off with any ridiculous story about delivering fireworks, because I know it isn't true.'

'I wasn't going to.' Casimir put the catherine wheels down on the side table next to the coffee cup. One slid out of the open end of the packet and fell onto the floor. 'I'm looking for Simeon. I thought perhaps he was with you. They said downstairs you had somebody with you.'

'I did. My aunt and cousin have come up from the country for the Christmas ball. They've gone back to their rooms for breakfast. I haven't seen Simeon since yesterday. Had you any particular reason for thinking he was here?' Ruth waited for him to answer. When he did not, she said, 'Casimir, please. I've just lied through my teeth for you. I can't tell you how what I've just said to my father is going to be taken out on me later. My life is difficult enough without this. Don't you think I deserve an explanation?'

'I've already given you one.'

'No, you haven't. You've told me you're looking for Simeon. You haven't told me why.'

'There isn't any why.' It was a woefully inadequate answer. Casimir could not keep the stubborn note out of his voice. 'After you quarrelled, Simeon went charging off. He didn't come back last night, or this morning. I thought he must have followed you here, to make up.'

'Well, he didn't. And if he did, I can assure you, my father would never let him spend a night under this roof. You surely can't have any trouble believing that.' She added, 'You don't have to look so pleased about it.'

'I'm not pleased about it.'

'No. And that's the problem, isn't it, Casimir? You've never been pleased. Even now, when Simeon is missing and there is obviously something going horribly wrong, you won't even permit me the privilege of being worried about him. Has it occurred to you I might have more influence than you give me credit for? That I might be able to help, if you only told me what was happening?

No. Because the fact is, you don't want me to help. You don't even want me to know where Simeon is.'

'You can't help with this.'

'How do you know?'

'Because I do.'

'You mean, because you don't want me to.'

'No, I mean, because I know you can't help. There are things you just don't understand,' said Casimir. 'What do you know about us, anyway? What do you know about Simeon? This time last year, you hadn't even met him. You can't help with what's happening because you don't know the first thing about our lives.'

'No? Well, that cuts both ways, doesn't it.'

'What do you mean?'

'It means,' Ruth said, 'that if I know comparatively little about your life, then you know nothing, *nothing*, at all about mine.' Abruptly, she got up and went to the door. When she had bolted it, she sat down again on the settle. 'How old are you, Casimir? Fourteen? Fifteen? I know you're at the end of your apprenticeship, because Simeon has told me. I don't suppose it's ever occurred to you to wonder what I was doing when I was your age, so let me tell you. I was married. When I was thirteen, my father, whom you have just met, and my mother, who, when she was alive was even worse, forced me to marry a fifty-seven year-old margrave who legally owned me as if I were a table or an acre of land. I was sent out to his estate on the outer limits of Osterfall, five hours from the nearest town. I knew no one. My husband was a brute. For the first six months I was so distraught I wanted to kill myself. I spent two years being gut-wrenchingly terrified, another three growing slowly numb to everything which surrounded me, and then ten being bored to the point of despair. All I had for company were my books and my husband's poor silly cousin, Tycho. Then a miracle happened. My husband died of a stroke and Princess Christina was called back to court by the Queen and offered me a place as her lady-in-waiting. If it were not for her, my father would long since have forced me into another sham marriage with yet another diseased and decrepit nobleman.

'Do you understand why I'm telling you this? It's because I want you to try and grasp why I am the way I am. You think I'm trying to steal Simeon away from you. Well, maybe I've unwittingly given you reason to think that, but the fact is that for the last nine months, I've seen your father maybe once a week, twice if I'm lucky. When he leaves Starberg, which I imagine he will quite soon, I will probably never see him again. That is how much I have had of your father's life, Casimir. Begrudge it to me if you will, but at least remember you can go with him. I can't. Compared to me, you are free as air.'

'I'm not free,' said Casimir. 'Nobody's really free. What Simeon says is a lie.'

'Maybe it is,' said Ruth. 'But at least he gave me hope, for a little while, and I'm grateful for that.'

'Simeon's not free, either,' said Casimir. 'What do you know? You don't even know what he really is. Simeon's a magician. He trained in black magic when he was a child and the man who attacked me in the park is the son of his old master. Simeon destroyed his father's memory and now Circastes is after him he's practising magic again. He killed someone to save me. Now you know why we're in trouble. What can you do to help?'

Ruth said nothing. She sat on the settle with her hands in her lap and looked at him. From the expression on her face Casimir could see she had guessed some or most of it, exactly how much, he did not know. She would have been stupid if she hadn't, for the clues had been there from the beginning. Nevertheless, the revelation had still hurt her, the way it had hurt Casimir himself in the same situation the day before yesterday. Yet he also sensed that, in a very real way, Ruth didn't care. To her, what Simeon was simply didn't matter; what cut deeply was the fact that he had not trusted her enough to confide in her. Casimir knew the reason why his father had not done this, that it was from concern for her safety, not lack of trust. Simeon had not wanted to draw Ruth to Circastes's attention. But Ruth did not know this. As far as she was aware, Simeon had simply kept her in ignorance because he did not want her to know.

'Casimir,' she said at last, 'if this performance is designed to antagonise me, you're going about it in completely the wrong way. I am not going to be manipulated like this. Whatever there is between you and Simeon is for you to sort out. Don't try and put your guilt on my shoulders. It's not my business. I am not your mother.'

'Yes, and I'm not your son.' As he said this Casimir suddenly realised why she annoyed him. Ruth expected him to act like an adult, but constantly put him in positions where it was impossible to behave like one; she not only treated him as if he was inadequate, she made him feel it. He stood up. 'You think just because you sleep with my father it gives you the right to tell me what to do. Well, it doesn't. You think I don't remember my mother, but I do. She had red hair, and she wore green sandals and played the guitar. She was beautiful and Simeon loved her. Who do you think you are, telling me what to do?'

He had gone too far. Ruth's face, which had gone white, then very pink, suddenly crumpled, and her eyes brimmed and overflowed with tears. She fumbled for a handkerchief, couldn't find one, and pointed to the door.

'Get out. Now. This minute. Leave this house, Casimir, and don't come back.'

Casimir went. There was no point in staying, or in apologising for what he had said. Nevertheless, he felt ashamed of himself. The only thing he could truly remember of Jessica and Simeon was the way they had quarrelled. In lying, he knew he had somehow diminished his mother even further.

Halfway back to Fish Lane, Casimir remembered the letter he had put in his pocket and pulled it out. He unfolded it, paused by a poulterer's shop where the Christmas birds in their bright plumage hung in the window, and read the first few sentences. The letter was dated Saturday morning, a few hours after the disastrous firework display, and was clearly an apology. Simeon had always expressed himself better on paper than in spoken words, but this was so direct and eloquent and painful, it was as impossible to read as it would have been to stand by and watch two lovers kiss. Casimir refolded it. As he did, he caught a glimpse of print on one of the underlying pages, and realised that he had picked up another letter as well.

The scrawled handwriting on the second letter was immediately familiar, though, since it was unsigned, it took Casimir a few moments to recognise it was the same as that on the letter Tycho had delivered yesterday. It was brief, an invitation to dinner at the Duck and Drake, and it enclosed a pamphlet. Casimir stood and read this through to the end. When he had finished, he put it back into his pocket and rejoined the throngs of people on the street. He still did not know where Simeon was. But a horrible suspicion was forming in his mind, and he knew that if he was right, Simeon was playing some deep and dangerous game of his own, and that he no longer knew what his father was capable of or not.

CHAPTER SEVEN

Casimir did not go back to Fish Lane. There did not seem to be any immediate point. He did not want to meet the man from the ordnance and the likelihood of Simeon's return seemed to be dwindling rapidly. Instead, he did what he often did when he wanted uninterrupted space around him. He went to the cathedral and sat in one of the deserted side chapels to think.

By the time he arrived, the service the queen had been attending was almost over. Casimir, who had forgotten about it, sneaked in by the west door through a reverberating cloud of brass music. A Household Guardsman looked askance at him as he passed, but otherwise nobody paid him any attention at all. Unlike most of the neighbouring buildings, the cathedral was truly ancient. King Frederik had not been especially interested in churches and had refrained from ripping it down during the great re-building program of the previous reign. But he had not spent any money on it either, and had stolen the best of its carvings for his new summer palace at Frederiksberg. As a result the great building was in a poor state of repair, and the chapel had been completely stripped. One wreath of greenery stood under a memorial to Carl-Frederik, the young brother of Margrave Greitz. Otherwise it was empty. Casimir liked it both for its scale and its unfussiness, and most of all for the fact that hardly anyone else went there. It was dark and cold and if he was quiet nobody was likely to find him, particularly today, when all the attention was focussed on the service just finishing in the main nave.

Casimir lit a candle to give himself some light and settled back in a corner where he could not be seen. Nearby, Carl-Frederik's memorial tablet told of a boy of exceptional promise (unpromising ones had a higher survival rate, thought Casimir cynically), who had died in mysterious circumstances twenty years before. His parents promised revenge against the enemy responsible for his death, sentiments which had always struck Casimir as uneasy for a tombstone, especially one in a church. Nevertheless, he supposed Carl-Frederik's parents had meant what they said. Gossip had always attributed the boy's death to the jealousy of Princess Christina's mother, Astrid, whose own downfall had followed not long afterwards. Casimir shifted his position so he did not have to look at the inscription. Given his own situation, the word 'revenge' had too many uncomfortable resonances.

His anger against Ruth was fading. Part of Casimir realised that, in antagonising her, he had just made a big mistake. When he had told her she could not help them, he had been thinking primarily of their dilemma with

Circastes. But the magician was not their only problem. Ruth had connections at court, and at the very least, she might have been able to find some way of stopping the ordnance snooping into their affairs. She could also have shed some light on the outrageous pamphlet Casimir had just discovered on her desk. Casimir took it out of his pocket and covertly re-read the first few paragraphs. The pamphlet was called 'On the Death of Monarchs', and there seemed something perversely apt in the act of perusing it here, with the queen herself just behind the great fluted pillars that separated the nave from the chapel. Casimir thought his uncle would have appreciated the irony, but while Joachim might have distributed the pamphlet if the stakes were high enough, even he would have been unlikely to have approved its contents. By its very nature, it had to be anonymous, but the confused ranting style had Tycho written all over it. Casimir did not wonder that Ruth had told him to burn Simeon's copy. The only wonder was, she had not yet burned her own.

According to the pamphlet, the government would soon be swept away by a glorious revolution. The queen, her cousin the procurator, and Princess Christina would all be assassinated and everyone would be free to do as they pleased. To help readers prepare, instructions followed on the use of firearms, the properties of gunpowder, and the manufacture of bombs. The author concluded by saying that, since only the briefest detail could be given in so short a work, the interested reader was referred to the treatise, *On Gunpowder and Explosives* by Simeon Runciman. Casimir, who knew his father had written just such a work at the request of the Comptroller of the Ordnance, felt sick at the thought of what this casual reference might imply for their safety. He could not believe that Tycho could be so stupid or irresponsible as to cite his father's name in such an openly seditious work. For Simeon was not, had never been a violent man.

Simeon did not believe in monarchs. He did not believe in any government save that of the individual conscience, which he believed to be the ultimate arbiter. But he was also a pragmatist used to living in the real world. He had never pushed his philosophies on anyone—the main reason he had never run foul of the Queen's Guard—and he had never advocated violence in order to put his ideas across. Simeon had had a bellyful of killing in the army; had seen too many good men blown to pieces for no real reason. To him, fighting was something one did because one had to, and was better left to professionals. Tycho's cork-brained incitement to revolution was about as far from his convictions as it was possible to get, and Casimir could not have believed his father would willingly have become involved with it, had he not already been acting so horribly out of character.

A thought that had been forming for some time on the edge of Casimir's consciousness came finally into focus. Ever since Circastes's attack on Friday night they had been waiting for the magician to return. Yet they had seen nothing of him. Suppose, though, the magician was already working out his threatened revenge? Suppose everything that had gone wrong since Friday night—the Queen's Guard, the ordnance man, and, most of all, Simeon's strange behaviour—was directly attributable to the magician's influence?

The music died and in the nave, Casimir could hear a blessing echoing richly off the vaulted walls. The response came back from the congregation, and then there was a recessional followed by rustlings and conversation growing slowly louder as the people attending the service dispersed. Casimir put the pamphlet back into his pocket and left the chapel. By the time he reached the nave the queen had gone. Her throne, a fanciful gilded structure draped with crimson silk and ermine, still stood on a dais near the pulpit. A smaller, less ornate throne stood beside it and its presence gave Casimir a moment's pause, for strictly speaking, he was sure Margrave Greitz had no right to sit on the dais until after he and the queen were married. He felt a twinge of unease. The political ramifications of the forthcoming royal wedding were something Casimir had not given a great deal of thought to. For the first time, perhaps because of the Queen's Guard's unwelcome interest in his own life, the trepidation felt by others on the matter seemed to have substance.

Across the aisle, the queen's musicians were packing up. Casimir went out into the cloister, where in winter there was a permanent soup kitchen, and lined up for a free bowl of thick broth and a chunk of black bread. The woman behind the pot looked at him suspiciously—he had pulled the trick before, and was too well-fed looking—but she handed him the food anyway, and he ate it ravenously. Simeon, who claimed not to believe in God and had never entered a church in Casimir's memory, would no doubt have ticked him off for taking food from the mouths of the poor. But Casimir was hungry, and this afternoon it occurred to him that a man who spoke with dread of tearing holes in the fabric of creation had no right to call himself an atheist anyway. If Simeon did not believe in God, it was probably because he had good reason to be afraid of him.

⁂

Casimir's next step was to try and find Tycho. After giving the matter some thought he went to Thursdays' print shop. It was a favourite haunt of his and Simeon's, a real bookshop with a reading room and library, that had somehow managed to beat the Queen's Guard and stay in operation. It had done this chiefly because its owners, Will and Annice Thursday, were not native Ostermarkans. Most of what they published was for export, and Will was a bad businessman, too interested in helping third rate writers to ever make his print shop thrive. Casimir knew him and Annice slightly. They were friends of Simeon's, and on Wednesdays, their half-closing day, he and his father went to read the books and newspapers in the reading room. The shop was also a meeting place for friends and gossips and one of Joachim's first ports of call when he came to Starberg in search of stock. It was also, appropriately enough, the place where Tycho and Simeon had met.

At the cathedral gate Casimir turned left instead of right, then right again. He passed under a low stone archway and emerged into a narrow court full of bookshops. *The Dolphin. . . The Courier. . . The Boar's Head Press*. From some of the shops came the muffled thuds and clanks of printing presses at work. Lead waterspouts in the shape of printers' devils dripped water onto the cobblestones and the puddles were stained black with ink. Halfway down the street a window with books and maps was surmounted by a green signboard:

W. & A. Thursday
Printers, Booksellers and Stationers
Circulating Library

Casimir pushed open the door and went inside.

There was nobody behind the counter, but a baby was crying upstairs and the workroom door was open. A man with a shaggy moustache was sitting at a table, setting type in a composing stick. Three printing presses were ranged about the room and damp sheets of paper were looped up like washing overhead. There were great trays of type, an ink-stained sink, and other equipment Casimir did not know the use of. Will lifted his hand when he saw Casimir and beckoned him in. When he had finished setting the line of type, he checked it against the written page he was working from and slid it from the composing stick into a metal tray.

'Hello, Cas,' he said. 'You've been making yourself scarce, lately. How can I help you?'

'Have you seen my father?'

'Not lately. But then, I've been busy. Baby's been keeping us on our toes.'

'Have you seen Tycho, by any chance?'

Will gave him an appraising look. 'Why?'

Casimir took the pamphlet out of his pocket and laid it briefly on the table. 'He gave us this. I want to speak with him about it.'

Will glanced at the paper. Casimir waited. It was a gamble, but someone had to have printed the thing, and Will and Annice were the obvious candidates. Will gave no sign of recognising the pamphlet but said, 'As a matter of fact, he's upstairs. He's been living in our garret for the last few weeks: Annice felt sorry for him and took him in. Up two flights, last door on the landing. Knock four times and he'll know it's a friend.'

'Thanks.' Casimir was not entirely sure he wanted Tycho's friendship, but it seemed churlish to say so. He went upstairs, found the door and knocked four times. A moment later a voice called out,

'Come in.'

Casimir opened the door.

Tycho's room was under the roof, an attic not unlike Casimir's own. It was better fitted out, though, with its own stove, clothes press, table and chairs. The great revolutionary had been making coffee on the stovetop and the milk had boiled over; a half-eaten lunch of bread, meat and cheese sat on the table and there was a stink of sour beer. The floor was covered with papers, books, dirty dishes and discarded clothes. Tycho himself was dressed in the same brown velvet outfit he had been wearing the day before, but with one difference: an empty sword belt was now slung over his shoulder. On the table lay the sword itself, a Spanish one with a fancy hilt. When he saw Casimir, he scowled.

'What are you doing here?'

Casimir looked up from the sword. 'I'm trying to track down my father. Have you seen him?'

'I might have done.'

'What does that mean?'

'Just that. I might have done. What makes you think I'd know where he is, anyway?'

Casimir hesitated. He had always thought of Tycho as a fool, but confronting him was not so easy as he had expected. Casimir was only fourteen, Tycho a grown man who, for all his folly, had an intimidating physical presence. There was also the sword on the table. Casimir did not imagine for a moment that Tycho would use it, but it did nothing to make him feel easy about what he had come to discuss.

'I came because of that letter you brought,' he said carefully. 'The one with the pamphlet in it.'

'I don't know what you mean.'

'Yes, you do. "On the Death of Monarchs".'

'Never heard of it.'

'Yes, you have. You came to the shop yesterday and gave me a copy for Simeon.'

'I told you that letter was for your father.'

It was a tacit admission, but Casimir knew better than to pounce on the fact. 'I know. But Simeon went charging off last night after he got it and he hasn't been back since. I thought he might have come to speak with you about it.' At this, Tycho said nothing. Sensing his close attention, Casimir pressed on, 'There's something you ought to know. Since Friday, the Queen's Guard has had men watching our house. They're suspicious about what happened. If Simeon's been taken in for questioning. . . '

For the first time, a genuine expression of alarm passed across Tycho's face. 'What do you mean, you're being watched? Your father never told me this!'

'So, you *have* seen him.'

'We spent the night talking at the Duck and Drake.'

'All night? What for?' Casimir felt a sort of grim presentiment; whatever excuses Tycho might come up with, if Simeon had spent the night talking with him, it had to be connected with the pamphlet. 'It was you who wrote that pamphlet, wasn't it? Why did you do it? Even my uncle wouldn't sell stuff like that. It's outright treason, he wouldn't be found with it in his pack.'

'Ha,' said Tycho, placing little confidence in Joachim's probity. 'I wouldn't be so sure about that if I were you. All right, I wrote the pamphlet. I'm not ashamed of it. Somebody has to say what they think. Somebody has to point out the obvious. What do you think is going to happen if that idiot, Elsabetta marries Greitz? She'll effectively hand control of the country over to the Queen's Guard, that's what. If you think life's difficult now, wait until we have the procurator sitting on the throne with his sweet little wife saying yes, dear, no dear, whatever you say. Let's trash the city, stamp on the thinkers, put all the scum like Tycho and his friend the firework maker into the Undercroft, and while we're on it, your dear sister Christina and her friend the margravine need husbands, let's find them some among my officers, they'll know how to keep them in check. Hand them all over to the interrogators, what's a few more corpses in the Ling; let's wade in blood through the streets of Starberg. Well, if you think I'm going to stand by and do nothing, you're wrong. There's no shame in killing a tyrant, and if I die, I would glory in it, glory, do you hear me!' Tycho's voice peaked in a shout. He banged his fist on the table, making the sword jump and Casimir jump, too. He found himself backing away a step. Tycho's reputation as a firebrand, a longstanding joke in the circles he mixed in, was suddenly starting to seem no longer funny.

'You're mad,' he said. 'You can't say things like that. You'll never get away with it.'

'You're wrong.' Tycho looked at him smugly. 'I have already.'

'What do you mean?'

'Nothing. None of your business. Why should I tell you anything, anyway?'

Casimir's frayed nerves snapped. 'Because I'm my father's son,' he shouted. 'And I care about my father. I care what happens to him, I'm afraid for him. I don't know what he's doing, but I want us to get out of this safely. And we're not going to do that if he's mixed up with a moron like you!'

Tycho's answer was to push back his chair. Suddenly Casimir realised how close his right hand was to the sword. His heart pounded, and he edged away.

'You know, you're a very rude boy,' Tycho said unexpectedly. 'It's easy to see why my cousin Ruth gets so upset. Frankly, I don't know why she puts up with you.'

'Nobody asked her to—'

'As a matter of fact, you're wrong. Your father did. And considering how much my cousin has done for you, you little filth, it wouldn't hurt you to be grateful—'

'Grateful?'

'—because where were you twelve months ago? Living off the back of a cart and sleeping under a haystack.' Tycho stood up and this time his stance was menacing. Casimir took a step back. 'What do you mean, coming in here like this? What do you mean, poking your nose into affairs that don't concern you, what do you mean, reading other people's letters? What do you—'

'All right, I'm leaving!' Casimir backed away until he hit the door. He pushed through it and ran down the stairs. As he passed the front room Will and Annice's baby started howling again, whether through hunger, wind, or simply the awfulness of having to live under the same roof as Tycho, Casimir did not know. He did not stop to enquire, but left the shop and went straight home. It did not occur to him immediately that in speaking to Tycho he might have acted unwisely, or that watching eyes might have taken note of his visit. But by the time it did, it was too late to have any regrets.

CHAPTER EIGHT

When Casimir returned to the shop he found Joachim gone, the firework boy missing from the window, and great gaps in the stock on the shelves. A cryptic note had been left for him on the counter. It said that Joachim had gone hunting and was signed after his uncle's fashion with three small circles to represent cannon balls. Soon after six o'clock Joachim came back, in a foul temper, for the rain had started up again, and he was sopping wet. Casimir was watching out for him from the shop. The lamplighter came and went; the rain drove in gusts along the cobbles. At last the street light was blotted out by a tall familiar figure in a topcoat. Its dark shape loomed in the window and there was a loud rap on the glass that sent the crocodile spinning on its string.

Casimir ran to pull back the fastenings. The door blew open, landing Joachim and a spatter of rain on the doormat. He thrust a greasy parcel into Casimir's arms.

'Merry Christmas,' he said sourly. 'Sorry about the goose. The poulterers were closed. This was all there was left.'

'I wouldn't know how to cook a goose if you gave me one,' said Casimir.

'You stuff it.' Joachim followed him out to the kitchen, where there was a fire going; he hung his topcoat on the back of the door and began removing his sodden clothing. His fingers ripped through the fastenings on his worn leather waistcoat and he draped a tattered scarf over the back of a chair. 'Which is what they ought to do to me, after this afternoon's effort. Four hours, following your father all around Starberg and what have I got to show for it? Not so much as a brass farthing. The magic's slipping. I must be getting old.'

Casimir opened the parcel and tipped a large, pungent sausage and some baked potatoes onto the table. 'You mean, Simeon came back?'

'Came back, closed the shop and went straight out again. He loaded up a handcart with fireworks and then took off. Furthermore, he did so right under the eyes of that ordnance officer, who came back at just the wrong time. Which leads me to something else, Casimir. Your father has magicked away the entire contents of the powder cellar. I don't know why, or where he's sent it, but when the ordnance man went down there to search, there wasn't a skerrick of black powder left, just a stink of magic that would have knocked out an elephant.'

Casimir's initial spurt of optimism fled. 'Where did Simeon go to?'

'Now that's the really interesting part,' said Joachim. 'Nowhere at all. At first he headed out as if he was going to the River Court, but he turned off before he got there. He went past the Undercroft, looped back up by the cathedral—past Fish Lane again—then down through the Christmas market by the Ling. All the time he was striding along, head down, as if he knew exactly where he was going. But in fact, all he was doing was marching around in a circle. People were starting to look at him as if he was crazy. Then, on the fifth time around, he disappeared.' Joachim shrugged. 'I can't say where he went, or even what he thought he was doing. Before he left, he told me he was delivering fireworks for a party. He sounded perfectly reasonable, which for Simeon is probably about as ominous a sign as you can get. Here, hand me that sausage. It's going cold.' Joachim pulled a knife out of his boot top and started hacking it into slices. 'God, this looks disgusting. Tough as shoe leather and five weeks old if it's a day. Another twenty-four hours and it'll come back to life. Do you think it's edible?'

'You bought it.'

'I wouldn't take that as a recommendation. You forget, I spent ten years in the army.'

'The potatoes are all right.'

'I'd rather get food poisoning than eat a vegetable. I think I'll stick to beer. Well, that's my daily report. Why not tell me some good news and cheer me up?'

'There isn't any good news,' said Casimir. 'Well, I suppose the mortars are all right. A bit damp, and they need cleaning, but they're safe. Apart from that, I found out where Simeon spent last night. He was with Tycho in the Duck and Drake.' He pulled Tycho's letter and 'On the Death of Monarchs' out of his pocket. 'Here. I stole this off Ruth. Tycho's sent copies to her and Simeon, other people too. The worst of it is, I think he means what he says.'

Joachim read the title and his eyebrows went up.

'I think I'm going to need another drink.' He drew two mugs of beer from the keg in the corner, lit another tallow candle, and settled down at the table to read. Casimir sat watching, drinking his own beer and eating his slice of the sausage. It was not quite as bad as Joachim had intimated, but it was bad enough that he could feel his stomach turning as he ate it. When he had finished, he ate a second potato and then a third. Joachim reached the end of the pamphlet and laid it down thoughtfully.

'How many copies of this are out there?'

'I don't know,' said Casimir. 'But he's taken the trouble to have it printed, so there must be a few. And he wrote it himself, he admitted it to me. He told me he would glory in it if he died.'

'He wouldn't if he'd ever seen action,' said Joachim dryly. 'Glorying in death doesn't sound like Simeon.'

'No. But Simeon's not been acting normally. Not since the firework display, when Circastes came back. And I'm starting to think I know why.' Casimir had now had several hours to think about it. 'Nobody takes Tycho seriously. He's an idiot. Normally, I can't think of anyone Simeon would be less likely to sit all night in a pub with. But suppose Circastes had got inside his head? Suppose he's driving Simeon, telling him to do what Tycho wants? It would explain why he's acting so strangely, why he's taking the gunpowder out of the powder cellar and the fireworks out of the shop. Because Simeon's help is all Tycho needs. Simeon has gunpowder, he has the mortars at Ruth's place and he knows how to use them. And the thing that really frightens me is that the queen's wedding is only two weeks away.'

'Maximum confusion. All the court and grandees of Ostermark in the same building,' said Joachim thoughtfully.

'Yes,' said Casimir. 'Why does Circastes have to kill Simeon, when he can force him to kill himself? And for a cause he doesn't even believe in. Or maybe he wants him to be arrested and executed. That would explain why Circastes attacked the firework display on Friday night. It brought Simeon to the attention of the Queen's Guard and they've been watching us ever since.'

'You may be right,' said Joachim. 'On the other hand, I doubt Circastes has waited for his revenge all these years without wanting to be in at the kill. Because I'm sure he does intend to kill Simeon. Not you. He has other plans for you, or he would have killed you outright on Friday night.' Joachim picked up the pamphlet. 'You're right: Tycho is an idiot. Unfortunately, he's also half right about this. Elsabetta is a fool, an intelligent well-meaning fool, which is the worst sort. This marriage is the most ill-advised thing she could have conceived. If Christina became queen, things might be different, but as it stands. . . I'm starting to wonder whether or not it would be worth my leaving Ostermark.'

'Leave Ostermark?'

'Why not? I wasn't born here. I don't owe the place anything. You could come too, if you like.'

'I couldn't. Not without Simeon.'

'We could meet up with Simeon, later,' said Joachim, but he saw from Casimir's expression what he thought and did not press the point. 'At the very least, Cas, we should think about leaving this house. Staying here is becoming too dangerous. If Tycho's been letter-dropping treason all over Starberg, you can bet a lucky seven on the fact that he's being watched. You would have been seen visiting him and so would Simeon. Pretty soon, somebody else is going to start and make the same connections you have and when that happens, our chances of evading arrest are going to be pretty slim.'

Casimir had not thought of this. 'Where can we go?' he asked helplessly.

'I'm not sure yet,' Joachim confessed. 'But before we do anything, I want to know more about what Simeon's been up to. Come with me. I want to look around upstairs.'

Casimir picked up the oil lamp. He did not bother to douse the fire. Since there were virtually no fireworks left in the building it hardly seemed to matter any more. His lamp glow cast eerie shadows over the walls as he followed his uncle up the stairs to Simeon's first-floor study. A stale smell of used magic fluttered out when they opened the door, like moths from an old woman's clothes chest.

'What are you looking for?' Casimir asked.

'Anything suspicious. Papers, magical apparatus. Simeon used to have a wand. It was made out of black wood, about the thickness of my thumb. Of course, it's possible he has it with him. I assume your father has the keys to this?' Joachim indicated the big chest under the window. When Casimir nodded, he produced a wire lockpick from his pocket and set to work with it. Casimir put the lamp down on the desk. Its single drawer contained pencils, quills and plain white paper, but underneath these was the tin gun case that had held their personal papers. To Casimir's surprise, the box was no longer empty. It now contained a sizeable bundle of letters on creamy paper, tied up with an old yellow hair ribbon.

Casimir lifted the letters out of the box. A small object fell out of one of the folds into his hand and he felt something lurch inside him. Lying in his palm was a fat, red curl, tied at the end with a silken thread.

The hair was glossier, thicker, perhaps a shade darker than his own. Casimir held the lock wonderingly between his fingers, marvelling at the fact that it even existed, that Simeon had kept it hidden all these years. Then Joachim looked up from the chest. With an oath, he crossed the room and plucked the curl from Casimir's fingers, lifted the mantle on the lamp and thrust it into the flame.

'What are you doing?' Casimir made a grab at the curl, then the letters, too late, for Joachim was already untying the bundle. Meanwhile the lock of hair sizzled, smoked, and flared away to nothing. Casimir felt a surge of rebellion and anger, mixed with disappointment so bitter he could almost taste it. Like all the other traces his mother had left of her existence, the token was gone before he'd had a chance to do more than register its presence.

'Simeon had no right to keep that,' said Joachim, curtly. 'A magician can do a lot with a piece of hair.' He removed the cover from the lantern and poked at the last charred shreds with a long, dirty finger. 'The chest's unlocked,' he added, and Casimir turned aside without a word. He could not bear to watch while Joachim opened and read, then cold-bloodedly destroyed his mother's letters one by one.

The chest held next to nothing to show for Simeon's life: just some books and a pair of flintlocks in a shagreen case, a military issue powder horn and shot pouch, and a few changes of clothes and bed linen. Casimir took them all out and stacked them neatly on the floor. At the bottom of the box was a false floor for hiding cash, removable by pressing a hidden spring in the side. There was no money in it tonight, though: only a bundle wrapped in a thin piece of black silk. Inside were the ebony wand he had seen Simeon using on the window, a squat black book like a small bible, and his father's copy of Tycho's letter, enclosing 'On the Death of Monarchs'.

'I've found the wand.'

'Good.' Joachim had finished burning the letters. He rubbed his fingers briefly through the ashes to make sure there was nothing left and took the bundle out of Casimir's hands. The book he glanced at briefly and set aside, but he picked up the wand with evident satisfaction and balanced it expertly in his hand. Then, before Casimir had a chance to anticipate his intentions,

125

he uttered a single guttural word under his breath and ran it swiftly along the wooden window frame.

There was a crackle and a flare as of a firework catching. At once the silver characters Casimir had seen Simeon inscribe there flared into life. Casimir almost dropped with shock.

'What are you doing?'

'I'm checking the wards Simeon's put up. Don't worry, I know what I'm doing. When one fraternises with magicians, one picks these things up.' Joachim finished his pass around the window. 'There'll be others, of course. Simeon will have put them on every window and door. I'm curious to see how thorough he's been.' As he spoke, a noise like a punch sounded somewhere below them. Casimir looked around sharply.

'What's that?'

'Sssh!' Joachim lifted his finger to his lips. He went to the door and stood there a moment, listening intently. Casimir listened too, but could hear nothing beyond the normal creaking of the wooden building. Joachim waited a few seconds longer. Then he abruptly extinguished the lamp and thrust the wand into Casimir's hand.

'Stay here.' He slipped through the door and went down the stairs. Casimir stood, obediently waiting beside the desk. After half a minute had gone past, he tiptoed out to the top of the stairs and stood listening in the darkness. A board creaked under his foot and his palms felt greasy with fear. Then he heard several sets of footsteps shuffling softly at the bottom of the staircase. There was a flash, as of a dark lantern briefly uncovered, and the tread of military boots on the staircase.

The sound broke Casimir's momentary paralysis. He thrust Simeon's wand into the waist of his breeches. Conscious he would have only a few seconds to make his escape, he turned and ran upstairs to the attic landing as lightly as he could.

Casimir opened the skylight and a blast of cold air and a spatter of rain came in. He grabbed the frame, its sharp edges excruciating against his bandaged hands, and swung himself up, once, twice. A voice sounded below and he heard footsteps on the stairs. On the third swing, no longer trying to be silent, he managed to hook a leg over the edge of the skylight and hauled himself, bodily upwards through the gap.

'Up here!' yelled a voice, and Casimir rolled over onto the roof and slammed the skylight shut. The slates sloped vertiginously away from him, black and slippery with water and streaked with bird droppings, without gutter or purchase of any kind. At the front of the building was the street and an impossible three-storey drop onto sharp cobbles; the back prospect was scarcely less alarming, with only the separate roof of the workroom to break his fall into their backyard. Casimir started scuttling sideways on his hands and bottom, aiming for the abutting roof of the neighbouring house. Then something crackled in his pocket and he realised with a jolt of horror it was Ruth's copy of Tycho's letter and pamphlet.

If he was caught with them in his possession, it could be deadly. Casimir dragged the papers out and started ripping them up as quickly as he could, driven by sheer terror and illogic, for he knew he should be escaping, not lingering where he would inevitably be taken prisoner. As he kept tearing, the amount of paper seemed to grow until it filled and overflowed his hands. Then suddenly there was a black hissing sound from his belt. Light surged from the wand and the pieces of paper flew up in a whirlwind around him, whipping his cheeks and blinding him in a miniature snowstorm of paper.

Casimir yelled and flung up his hands, slipping on the tiles. The skylight flew back with a crash and a man's head emerged.

'Stop right there!' He lifted a gun and fired it. The sound of the shot whizzing past his ear sent Casimir into a panic. He yelled again, lost his grip and started sliding on his backside down the roof, his booted feet struggling against the slate for any kind of purchase. Sparks flew up from his heels like stars from a grindstone and there was a whoosh of golden rain from the seat of his trousers. Then, like a small comet blazing earthward he slipped off the edge and fell with a thud onto the separate roof of the workroom.

The slate cracked and sagged. Casimir grabbed at a hole and missed it; he flopped over on his stomach and continued to slide, his fingernails scratching silver sparks up from the slates. In another second he had slipped off the edge into space, banging his head as he went over and almost knocking himself out. It was a jarring nine-foot drop into the yard. Casimir hit the ground and slipped over. There was a loud bang, like a salute going off, and the kitchen door flung open and half a dozen men came pouring out of the house.

'Stop!'

But Casimir did not stop. Somehow, he did not know how, for he was sure such a fall should have broken at least an arm or a leg, he was on his feet and running for the yard gate. One hand grasped the latch and threw it open, and he was out and pelting down the mews behind Fish Lane. By now, he knew he was running for his life. The lane was filled with obscuring smoke, the smell of gunpowder inextricably mingled with magic. There was a hissing overhead and a flare of light, and down through the smoke, from the eaves of the houses and stables, a tunnel of gold and silver rain started falling around him. Casimir pulled Simeon's wand from his belt and tried to hurl it away, but it seemed glued to his palm and he could not discard it. Military boots thudded against the cobbles and he saw the red-flashed uniforms over his shoulder. Again there was a flash, a roaring stink of gunpowder, and this time he felt something red-hot pass through his body. Casimir stumbled, but only for a moment. He kept on running, somehow knowing that the shot had passed right through him and that any moment he would fall to the ground, spouting blood, and go spiralling down to his death.

But he did not. Instead the fireworks faded behind him. Now he could see his fingers lengthening, straightening, changing colour before his eyes, turning into bound bunches of red crackers that protruded from his red and blue-striped sleeves. Their tips burst into life, spitting pops and sparks; his hair stood on end and burned like coloured matches, and his eyes spun around like catherine wheels. He was no longer Casimir

Runciman, but the firework boy, and another shot would send him exploding into a thousand stars to light up the rainy night.

Then, on the street corner opposite the cathedral he saw Circastes.

The magician was barefoot and dressed in the same dark clothes he had been wearing on Friday night. He was sheltering under the eaves of a building and the men pursuing Casimir seemed not even to notice he was there. Casimir saw him draw back into the shadows and thought what fools they had been to even think he was gone away. He veered away, out into the street, and was relieved when the magician made no attempt to hold him back.

Across the road was the cathedral, its dark windows illuminated by pinprick lights, comfortingly familiar in the darkness and the rain.

Casimir pelted across the street and through the gate. Abruptly the fireworks vanished and he was dressed in his own drab, woollen winter clothes again. He rounded the corner of the building, and, in the shadow of the western cloister, saw the soup kitchen he had visited earlier in the day. Two men, one middle-aged and burly, the other one young and bearded, were dishing out meals and blankets, directing newcomers to spaces where they might sleep among those already dossed down for the night. Casimir darted through the iron gate into the cloister. The young man with the beard took one look at him, heard the running footsteps of his pursuers, and threw him a blanket from the pile. Casimir dived into the press of mummied bundles and the crowd silently opened and engulfed him, another anonymous refugee from authority.

He hunkered down, panting, under his blanket and buried his face between his knees. His palms were throbbing and sweating and he could barely catch his breath. Casimir wondered briefly what had happened to Joachim, whether he had been taken prisoner or somehow managed to escape. Then he heard the iron cloister gate creak open and knew the men from the Queen's Guard had followed him in.

Booted footsteps sounded. A voice spoke and was answered firmly. Casimir could not hear what was being said, but it was clear his pursuers were asking whether he had passed this way. A couple of guards started picking their way through the blanketed huddles, looking for a telltale shock of dark red hair. The elderly woman next to him reached out her hand for his. Casimir took it gratefully and looked up. There, sitting swathed in a blanket not three feet away from him, was Circastes.

There was a sharp tug at his waist, and Simeon's wand shot like a projectile out of his belt into the magician's hand. With a great shout, Casimir jumped to his feet. A brazier went over, showering sparks and burning charcoal over the pavement, and someone screamed, knocked down, or burned by a flying coal.

Casimir started scrambling towards the gate, but legs, bodies and the general confusion tripped him up. Three men in the uniform of the Queen's Guard started after him, and a fourth, standing by the soup pots, aimed a gun and tried to fire.

'Watch out!' The young man with the beard grabbed the marksman's arm, and the shot ricocheted off the stonework. Headed off by the other men, Casimir changed direction and ran for the cathedral door. His feet stamped on hands, bodies, legs, and then, just as he reached the soup pots, a guard caught up with him and grabbed his jacket. Casimir could feel his arm being dragged out of his sleeve, he could see the open door behind the cookpots and the brazier, and sense the pulling quietness beyond. Then help was with him. A couple of sturdy vagrants rose from the pavement, wrestling with the guards and pulling them off him. In the confusion of the struggle one of the vagrants was knocked over, screaming. Casimir heard steel drawn. The bearded man shouted a warning. He grabbed a guard by his red-slashed sleeve and the man swung around, sword in his hand. Then, so quickly Casimir scarcely saw it happen, the blade passed through the young man's body and he fell sprawling, blood gushing out of his mouth onto the cloister pavement.

With a howl the crowd of homeless people erupted upward, shouting and babbling in a free-for-all of panic. Casimir saw the guard with the sword go down in the melée, but by then he had yanked free and was through the door and into the cathedral. His feet rang out on the flagstones and a few worshippers looked up from the pews. The last service was over, the midnight vigil yet to begin; there was only a handful of people praying in the entire building. Casimir ran for the opposite entrance, but the great wooden doors were closed and barred. There was nowhere he could hide and after the long pursuit from the firework shop he was tired and at the end of his physical and mental resources. For a second he remembered something he had seen on a previous visit: a sparrow, which had flown in through a door, flying frantically back and forth in the vaulted dimness, twittering anxiously and beating itself up against a stained-glass window. Without hope of escape, but merely from desperation, Casimir threw himself under a pew. His pursuers caught up with him. One seized him by the ankles and pulled him roughly out. He rolled over, flailing, fighting them, and then there was a smashing blow on his head and his flight was over.

CHAPTER NINE

Casimir was asleep. His head ached and he was deathly cold, but though he tried repeatedly to stir himself he could not wake up. Three or four times he drifted close to the verge of consciousness and then ebbed away again, there was a roaring in his ears and his cheek seemed to be resting in something fetid and sticky. But at last the smothering darkness fled away and left him stranded. He was awake. A bag or length of heavy cloth was draped over his head and shoulders, and he was lying trapped in a stinking mess of half-digested sausage and baked potato.

The smell was nearly enough to make him vomit all over again. Casimir tried to move his hand. The movement sent hammer blows shooting up his neck into his skull; he heard the clank of manacles and could barely lift his arm from the weight and his own weakness. Underneath him was a rough stone floor. As he realised this, wild, hallucinatory images started flashing through his head. Circastes had come back. The Queen's Guard had come to the firework shop. His recollections were confused and patchy and he couldn't remember what had happened at the end, but it was obvious he had been taken prisoner. Which meant there was only one place he could be.

The Undercroft.

The word arced through Casimir's fuddled brain. In its wake came a kind of numb horror. That this had happened to him was more than he could comprehend. He hadn't *done* anything, and he was only fourteen, he hadn't even lived yet. Then it came to him that at some point in the next twenty-four hours he was probably going to die and he thought he had never known such aching despair. All the stories and half-whispered rumours he had ever heard about the Undercroft and the Queen's Guard came back to him: the tales of tightly bound bodies, found floating mysteriously in the river, of prisoners locked up for years without reason, and the mysterious chute that the torturers supposedly used to dispose of their victims into the Ling. Why should he survive in a place where so many went in and so few came out alive? Tears gushed down Casimir's cheeks and his nose ran until he could scarcely breathe in the confines of the sack. He struggled weakly against the material, and at last, with a great blubbering gasp, he succeeded in pulling it over his head.

At once he found he could breathe better. After the bag, the air in his cell was not as dank or stale as he might have expected; there was no filth or ordure from a previous occupant, and the only thing that really stank was him. Casimir lay down on top of the sack, crying and shivering, for it was bitterly cold, and he was inexplicably missing his jacket and shirt. A faint, a very faint glimmer of artificial light showed under what was obviously a door, and gave him a glimpse of his surroundings. There was no chair, no bed, no bucket in the cell—which immediately made him wish there was one—nothing to eat, nothing to drink, and not so much as a flea-ridden blanket to huddle in. The only thing he could hear was the sound of his own sobbing breath and the occasional rattle of his manacles as he shook from the cold.

After a while he heard footsteps and voices approaching. The door opened and two guards wearing the familiar red-slashed uniform came into the cell. The light from their lantern pierced Casimir's eyes. He flinched away, trembling.

'What a brave fellow,' said the first guard sarcastically. 'Dear me. Look at him. And nothing's even happened, yet.'

'Doesn't look much like a revolutionary, does he? Are you sure he's the one?'

'Too bad if he's not. Come along, firework boy. There are people who want to talk to you.' The guard dragged Casimir to his feet. He felt his legs wobble and give way; an excruciating pain shot through his head and subsided to a vicious pulse as the man swore and hoicked him up again. Manacles clanking, he was half-led, half-carried from the cell. Then the door closed behind him and he was marched away into darkness.

The Undercroft was not, strictly speaking, a prison. It had started life as a granary, owned by the Crown, but had long ago been converted to military usage. As the Queen's Guard had grown in size and power, attendant buildings had sprung up around it so that there was now an entire complex of barracks and storerooms. Casimir was taken up some stairs and then briefly into a small high-walled courtyard, where he saw the stars peeping mistily through a veil of cloud; he was then pushed through a door into another building and up some more stairs into what seemed to be a suite of offices. At the third door, one of the guards knocked and a man came out. He was wearing a uniform with more red on it than usual and he had a key and a gold quizzing glass on a looped chain around his neck.

'Ah, yes. The firework boy. Wait a moment.' He turned and went inside. Casimir could hear him talking to someone. Then a voice called out and he was shown into a room with high walls, a small window, and a long wooden table in the middle.

A fire was burning and the shutters were closed, there was a carpet on the floor and a jug of wine and some goblets on a side table. Casimir's first impression was that the room was full of people. Then his own escort withdrew to the passage, and he realised there were in fact only five men there, two of whom were guards. At the central table sat two men. One was writing on a sheaf of paper and was plainly a secretary. The second wore no uniform and sat in a slightly larger chair. He had dark brown hair, unusual in Ostermark, which he wore cut shorter than the fashion, and a neatly trimmed beard that was starting to turn brindle. One grey eye drooped slightly. Casimir thought he might be about Simeon's age, or a little older. Unbidden, a recollection of the obscene picture of Margrave Greitz he had seen amongst Joachim's papers popped into his head. He thought the likeness was far better than he might have expected.

On the table was a pile of old clothes: a brown jacket, shirt, and two grubby, woollen undervests. It took Casimir a few moments before he realised they were his own. In a separate pile were several other familiar objects. Simeon's black book from the trunk, Tycho's letter and 'On the Death of Monarchs'.

The man with the quizzing glass whispered to the procurator, then sat down beside him. The procurator turned to Casimir and spoke.

'Do you know who I am?'

Casimir did not say anything. The procurator waited a moment, then answered his own question in a soft, clear voice. 'I think you do. You may be surprised to see me here. Of course, I have a particular interest in this matter. I am always interested to meet people who want to kill me. Who else is implicated, Cassel?'

The man with the quizzing glass produced a list. 'In custody: Joachim Leibnitz, a foreigner of no fixed abode, ex-Ostermark artillery. Graff Marcus Tycho, formerly of Osterfall, now resident in Starberg. William Thursday, printer, a foreigner resident in Starberg. His wife Annice, foreigner, resident in Starberg. Casimir Runciman, apprentice, a foreigner resident in Starberg. Under house arrest: Ruth, Margravine Winterhalten, a native Ostermarkan formerly of Osterfall, now of Starberg. Still at large, Simeon Runciman, firework maker, ex-Ostermark artillery, foreigner resident in

Starberg. There are others under surveillance we have not yet taken in.'

'So.' The procurator turned back to Casimir. 'Conspiracy. Treason. The black arts. Not a bad collection of misdemeanours for someone of your age. There's also the matter of the scene you created in the street, and the priest who was killed at the cathedral when you were taken prisoner. I regret that. Our relations with the church are bad enough already. All in all you've caused me a lot of trouble. I'm not disposed to be lenient, but it would greatly help your chances if you were prepared to talk.'

'Begin with this.' Cassel picked up the jacket and tossed it at Casimir. He fumbled and caught it awkwardly in his manacled hands. The jacket was one of Simeon's, cut down to fit last winter and now too small for him. Casimir turned it over, suppressing a desire to drape it around his shoulders, for he was still very cold. He did not entirely understand the question, for as far as he could see, it was just a jacket. Then his searching fingers found it: a neat round hole in the middle of the back where the lead shot had pierced the cloth. There was a matching one on the front where it had exited, but not a drop of blood, or anything to explain how he had survived what should have been a fatal shot.

Casimir looked at his shirt lying on the table. The same perfect circle showed on the front, the linen slightly scorched around the edges. He felt his bowels begin to grind. There are degrees of terror, Joachim had once said to him. You really know you've hit rock bottom when you've shat yourself. That's what it's like at the start of a battle. Thousands of men lined up, all filling their breeches: you can smell it, it's disgusting. Casimir hauled on his muscles and clamped his legs together.

'If you can't explain, perhaps we can help you.' The procurator produced a dagger from his boot top and leaned across the table. He pointed its tip to Casimir's chest, at a new, small pink scar, slightly to the left of his breastbone. 'Care to tell us how you survived it?'

'I don't know.'

'Really?' The dagger hovered, brushing against the skin. Casimir closed his eyes and shook his head. Suddenly the point of the blade pricked into him. He yelled and jerked away, but the guard behind him grabbed his shoulders and stopped him dead. A trickle of hot blood welled up and coursed down his chest. He opened his eyes and saw Cassel and the procurator looking at him.

'There's a matching scar on your back,' said Greitz. 'If you like, we could mark that out for you, too. Alternatively, I could just push a little harder next time and see if you can repeat the trick. Maybe you'd better start and answer our questions. Where is your father?'

'I don't know.'

'Don't know's not good enough. Again, where is your father?'

'I don't know, I don't know!' Casimir shouted, and then to his horror what he had dreaded actually happened: his body betrayed him. A great hot torrent of urine flooded down his legs, soaking his breeches and splashing the carpet. He could not believe how much there was of it. Across the table he saw the procurator's lips twitch. He and Cassel exchanged glances, and the little secretary smirked. They were laughing at him, actually laughing at him, and there was nothing he could do except stand there, dripping on the carpet. If Casimir could have died of humiliation and terror, he would have done so at that moment.

'Where is your father?'

'I don't know. I haven't seen him since Sunday morning. Please. Believe me, I'm telling you the truth!'

'Your father is a magician.'

'No.'

'He was seen practising magic on Friday night. He had a grimoire in his house, it's there on the table. Let me ask you again: is your father a magician?'

'Maybe. Once. I don't know.'

'Then you are a magician also.'

'No. It doesn't work like that.'

'How does it work, then?'

'I don't know.'

'You don't know much at all. Do you know what punishment the statutes prescribe for those who practise magic?' Casimir did, but was clearly not expected to answer. 'Burning. It's not a particularly common crime. The last case to come to trial was about fifty years ago. They used to do the burnings in the old market place down by the Ling. The magician was usually drugged so he could not use his magic. They chained him to a stake and soused him with pitch, and if they were feeling kind, they hung a bag of gunpowder around his neck before they set the flames going. Seems an appropriate end for a firework maker's apprentice. Burned on his own bonfire with a couple of loads of catherine wheels thrown in for good effect.'

'I'm not a magician,' said Casimir sullenly.

'I'm sure you're not,' said Greitz. 'If you were, I doubt you'd be standing here. But somebody was working magic when you fled your father's shop. Somebody your father is working with—'

'No!'

'—somebody who pretends to share your father's political opinions. Your father is a notorious radical. He has been under surveillance ever since you came to Starberg. He does not believe in governments, he wants to destroy the established order—'

'No.' Somehow Casimir gathered his shattered wits. 'My father doesn't want to destroy anything. He thinks that in time, people will learn for themselves, that they will come around to his way of thinking of their own accord.'

'That's not what it says in this pamphlet.'

'That was given to him. Simeon didn't ask for it, he doesn't believe it. He believes in people, and their right to choose. He believes that they have a right to be free and not oppressed by governments. He believes in everyone's right to live peacefully, without war or persecution or hardship. He believes,' Casimir's voice grew stronger, 'that if everyone behaved like this the world would be a better place. He might be wrong. He probably is. He hopes that human beings will be better and wiser than they really are or ever can be. But if he is wrong, at least his ideas have never hurt anybody. At least he is sincere.'

'Sincere enough to write a treasonous poem calling Her Majesty a tyrant?'

'No.' After months spent listening to chunks of *The Tyrant* read out loud during its composition Casimir knew it as well as if he had written it himself. Greitz had not read the poem. There had been no copies in the house when it was raided, and even if he had seen it elsewhere, he had wilfully misunderstood its message. He quoted Simeon. 'The tyrant is not a person, or a government or an external power of any kind. It is the binding spirit in all of us which will not let us do what we desire or achieve what we hope for.'

'And what does your father hope for? My death? Her Majesty's? That's what the pamphlet says, doesn't it? Let me read it to you: *That the existence of a monarchy is the Vilest Impediment to a man's exertion of his right to Choose, and that the Death of Monarchs, by violent means if necessary, is both Justifiable and Desirable, is a fact few sensible men will dispute. Assass—*'

'No! I've already told you, it wasn't Simeon! Tycho wrote it, not my father.'

'Graff Tycho wrote the pamphlet. Note that down,' said Greitz, and Casimir felt the words curdle in his mouth. In his anxiety to protect Simeon, he had forgotten that Tycho, too, was a prisoner. The man was a fool, and had brought this disaster down on all of them, but Casimir would not deliberately have incriminated him for the world. Greitz continued, 'As a matter of fact, we have been watching Graff Tycho for a while. We're reasonably certain of a lot of things. We know, for example, that the pamphlet was printed by William Thursday. The typefaces match those found in his printery. Then there is Joachim Leibnitz, known as a courier with subversive leanings, recently arrived in Starberg and taken prisoner. Your father is a known confederate of both these men. It is also known that a quantity of gunpowder has been removed from your premises in Fish Lane. Do you know where your father is?'

'No.'

Suddenly Greitz changed tack. 'You went to see the Princess Christina yesterday morning, I think. Is that correct?'

'I . . .' The change of tack took Casimir by surprise. 'Yes.'

'With your father?'

'No.'

'But your father saw her.'

'Yes. Ruth—Margravine Winterhalten took him.'

'But you went separately. What did the princess say to you?'

Casimir hesitated. Partly, it was from a sense that he was on dangerous ground, but he also found he simply couldn't remember exactly what had been discussed. It was as if a dark curtain had descended over his memories of the interview. He groped for something suitable to say. 'She—Her Highness told me she was concerned about the accident on Friday night.'

'Why?'

'Because she was at the display. She might have been killed. She thought the accident must have happened because Simeon was under strain. She told me to watch out for him. And if he did do anything, she told me . . .' his mind went momentarily blank and then the answer came to him in a flash from nowhere, 'she told me you would need to know at once. Because you were in charge and she was afraid the security for the wedding might be compromised.'

Greitz looked displeased. Casimir waited uneasily. Cassel, who had been sitting throughout the entire conversation, silently playing with his quizzing glass, now lifted the glass slightly as if conveying some unspoken warning, and with a flash of insight Casimir realised this matter encroached on something more dangerous and with wider implications than those that immediately affected him and Simeon. He wondered what the procurator really wanted from him, and who he was ultimately chasing. He was sure it was not him, and possibly, it was not even Tycho or Simeon. He remembered what Princess Christina had said to him: *My future brother-in-law learned to hate me when we were both still children.* Could it be that the person the procurator was hoping to incriminate was the princess herself?

The procurator sat a moment longer, considering. Then he turned unexpectedly to the two guards who had waited throughout the interrogation.

'For the moment, I think that will be all,' he said. 'Take him back to his cell. We'll decide what to do with him later.'

alone in his cell, Casimir wrapped the sack around his naked shoulders and curled up in the corner. The interrogation could have been much worse, but he did not imagine for a moment they had finished with him. They had not hurt him or pushed very hard with their questioning; all they'd really done was frighten him. They were softening him up for next time. Casimir did not delude himself that his chances of surviving intact until morning were anything but extremely slim.

Hours passed. Casimir dozed off briefly once or twice, but his aching head and trepidation about what was coming kept him from falling into a deep sleep. Eventually he was roused by the sound of the door being opened. It was Cassel, this time without his quizzing glass, accompanied by a guard carrying Casimir's clothes.

'Get dressed.'

The guard threw Casimir's clothes at his feet, then proceeded to unlock his manacles. Casimir picked up his vests and pulled them over his head, then put on his shirt and jacket. The guard opened the door and he was marched out down the corridor he had passed along earlier. This time, instead of turning left, his escort went right and led him up a flight of steps to a heavy, wooden door.

The guard opened it and a blast of wintry air hit Casimir's cheeks. With a shock he realised he was looking at Quay Street, the road that ran along the Ling towards the River Court. It was still night, still raining. A gleam behind the clouds showed the waning moon, setting over the water.

'You're a lucky boy,' said Cassel. 'The procurator has decided to release you. The printer's wife broke under questioning half an hour ago. She's told us all we need to know. For the moment, and I stress, for the moment, you're no longer wanted. As long as you don't attempt to leave Starberg, you're free to go.'

Casimir stared at him. He took a few unsteady steps forward, then looked back to see whether anyone was following. The great oak door of the Undercroft was already closing in his face.

Casimir walked down the steps into the street. The rain spattered his face and he turned up his collar. For the first time in his life, the endless Starberg winter drizzle seemed a blessing beyond price or compare.

CHAPTER TEN

Casimir was not even halfway home when he realised they had let him go. It did not take any particular insight or brilliance to reach this conclusion. A scratch on the chest, a wet pair of trousers, an interrogation that had comprised mere threats and menace, and they had turned him loose. He was on a leash and they were waiting to see in whose direction he would run.

Annice Thursday had broken under questioning. Casimir did not care to think what this had involved, or even if she and Will were still alive. Unlike Ruth, who had a toughness and emotional integrity that would be slow to break under pressure, Annice was soft and gentle. Furthermore, she had no one to protect her. She was just a printer's wife, a person of no particular importance who, like her husband, could disappear in an eyeblink without anyone daring to comment. And Joachim was the same. This realisation came to Casimir as something of a shock. Of course he had always known his uncle talked himself up, spinning tales that would have boggled the minds of anyone credulous enough to believe them, but the thread of truth that ran concealed through the weft of his fictions was such that he had nevertheless thought of him as somehow indestructible. Yet the truth was, Joachim was just a man who could die or be murdered as easily as any other. If Casimir was going to find Simeon, elude Circastes and get out of Starberg, he was now going to have to do it without his uncle's help.

Casimir turned into Fish Lane. He could not think of anywhere better to go, for he had no hiding place and there was always the chance—though rapidly diminishing—that Simeon would come back there. Halfway down the street he saw two men and a woman walking towards him. The men were carrying a set of familiar wooden chairs and the woman pulled a trolley laden down with household goods. As it trundled under a street lamp, he recognised Simeon's big pewter chamberpot filled to the brim with catherine wheels, crackers and jumping jacks.

'Hey! What are you doing?' Twenty-four hours earlier Casimir had been resigned to leaving everything behind, but the sight of his earthly possessions being carried off by a bunch of strangers brought an abrupt reversal in this thinking. He made an unsuccessful grab at the trolley. The chamberpot fell off with a crash and several jumping jacks exploded deafeningly inside it. 'That's ours—what are you doing?'

'Get lost!' The bigger of the two men grabbed Casimir's coat and gave him a shove that sent him skittering backwards. 'Mind your own business and you might stay in one piece.'

'I am minding my own business! You're stealing my things!' Casimir saw his own clothes, blankets and the striped pillow from his bed bundled up among the goods on the woman's trolley. The pillow struck a chord of panic, for it was the one into which he had sewn Princess Christina's gold ring. He snatched at the pillow, sending shirts, vests and stockings tumbling into the puddles. This time the man wrenched Casimir around, and dealt him a punch that missed his face, but caught him a glancing blow on the shoulder. Casimir's foot twisted and he lost his balance; the man caught him by the collar and sent him spinning forward into the overhang of a nearby house. He hit the wall with a thump and fell down on the cobbles with the pillow clutched to his chest.

Casimir groaned and rolled over, exaggerating his distress. To his relief, the scavengers paid him no more attention. They continued to the end of the street and disappeared around the corner. When they had gone, he got up and hurried to the shop.

A dispiriting sight awaited him. Someone had broken the glass on the street lamp outside their door and the red and gold signboard with Simeon's name on it had been wrenched from its fitting. When he stepped over the threshold he almost tripped over a sheet, filled with spoons, pewter plates, and household linen.

'*Shit*.' Casimir kicked the sheet and sat down disconsolately on the floor. With the exception of the sheet, which someone had obviously dropped in a hurry at his approach, the building had been completely stripped. Even the shelves which had been nailed to the walls were gone.

Casimir hooked his fingers into the ragged stitching at the end of the pillow and ripped it open. It took him a while to find the princess's ring sewn in among the feathers, but at last he fished it out and put it on. It fitted snugly on his little finger, a woman's ring with its raised pattern of roses circling the delicate gold band. Report back to me, the princess had said. Tell me if your father's behaviour gives cause for concern. Since their conversation, Simeon's behaviour had done little else, but that he might inform Christina of the fact had never crossed Casimir's mind for a moment. He could not believe it had seriously crossed the princess's, either. She could hardly have expected him to incriminate his own father.

At the very least, the princess's motives were unclear. The procurator, on the other hand, clearly smelled treason, and was trying to draw a line of connection between Christina, Simeon, and Tycho's plot. Casimir did not seriously believe there was one: after all, Christina had been named in Tycho's pamphlet as someone who was to be killed. But it still did not explain why she had been so willing to invite suspicion by ordering Casimir to the palace in the first place, or why she was so interested in his and Simeon's activities.

He could not trust her, for she was playing her own game, and he was also afraid of her. But there was now, quite literally, nobody else to go to. Around a quarter to seven, when the first grey gleams started penetrating the windows, Casimir let himself out through the skylight

151

onto the roof. He walked the length of Fish Lane, eventually jumping down into Cathedral Street via an outhouse roof. From there, he made his way as quickly as he could to the palace.

When he reached the River Court, it was still early in the morning. The princess's ring saw him safely past the sentry; lights burned in the palace windows and the air was raw as he pounded the great iron knocker on the western door. Fortunately Princess Christina was an early riser. The footman looked him over distastefully when he presented his credentials, but made less of a fuss about admitting him than Casimir had anticipated.

'Your business?'

'The princess will know what I'm here for.'

'Her Royal Highness. You'll have to do better than that if you expect an audience.'

'Just show Her Highness the ring,' snapped Casimir, and to his immense surprise the man turned and went clicking off down the polished corridor. Several minutes later he came back, carrying a set of dark, severely cut clothes over one arm. The coat was too long and the stockings too short; they made Casimir look like a page and were not new or even clean. But they were so much better than the stinking garments he was wearing that he could have almost cheered with relief.

'Use this.' The footman produced a comb and watched while Casimir made a futile attempt to drag it through his vomit-stiffened curls. When he had finished, the footman pointed for him to throw it into the fire and handed him over to a gentleman usher, who showed him upstairs into a pleasant sitting room. A fire burned in the hearth and vases of heavily scented flowers stood about on gilt stands, slightly drooping in the heat. The effect, in deep rose pink and gold, was like an expensive hothouse designed for a single, very beautiful exotic plant.

'Wait here. Her Royal Highness will be with you shortly.'

Casimir nodded, and the man withdrew. He took a step forward, his feet sinking deep into a luxurious carpet. Family pictures lined the walls: the queen in several poses, the late king, a crayon sketch of a smiling, adolescent Christina with her arms around the neck of a woman with a vaguely familiar face. Then, almost hidden behind a vase of flowers he saw a hinged miniature. On a whim, he picked it up and opened it out. It showed a young woman, perhaps aged no more than twenty, with dark ringlets worn in the fashionable beribboned style of the last generation. She was wearing a low-cut, lustrous gown, and around her neck on a length of black velvet ribbon was a diamond pendant in the shape of a many-rayed star.

Astrid. Oster. Regina.

The name was written, in the old fashioned way, in tiny gold letters in the top right-hand corner, and confirmed by the star pendant, with its visual pun on her name. The queen's bold, black eyes stared out at Casimir across twenty-five years and made him blush. He had heard that King Frederik had destroyed all his wife's portraits after her mysterious death, because he could not bear to be reminded of her. This one must have survived because it was so tiny, scarcely bigger than a locket. Curiously, Casimir looked from the miniature to the picture of the woman embracing Christina, and this time he immediately saw the family resemblance. While Christina's blonde beauty did not recall her mother in the slightest, the other woman looked sufficiently like Queen Astrid to be identified as a sister or some other near relation.

Yet that did not explain his sense of recognition when he had first seen the crayon portrait. Christina's companion — aunt? — had reminded him of someone else, but he did not know who it was. Suddenly, as he had on Friday night at the disastrous firework display, Casimir felt a strange sensation of something being closed off inside his head. He put the picture down and moved away from the table. The doorknob turned with a click behind him and the princess came, alone and unannounced, into the room.

She was wearing a grey silk wrap with deep sleeves and an embroidered train, a garment which Casimir guessed would have passed in a lesser mortal for a dressing gown. As yet, she was unmade-up, and her damp hair exuded clouds of an expensive floral perfume. Too late, Casimir remembered he was supposed to bow. The princess sat down and arranged the folds of her gown carefully around her feet. She looked him over coldly and said,

'I hope this is urgent. My Aunt Paulina has had a stroke and is likely to die. She reared me, you know, after my mother died. I will be leaving for Osterfall within the hour, so you had better make this quick.'

'It *is* urgent,' said Casimir. 'Circastes has come back. He's got my father under his control.' As he said it, his

154

emotion and the ordeal of the previous night got the better of him. His voice cracked, and, to his utter humiliation he broke down in tears.

'Calm down,' said Christina sharply. 'You're not a child, to be crying like this.'

'I can't. I can't help it.'

'You can. You must. Casimir, if you don't stop crying I shall send downstairs for some servants and have you beaten, and don't think I don't mean what I say because I do. Now, tell me what's happened, slowly. And don't leave anything out.'

She did not ask him to sit down. Sobered by her threats, Casimir pulled himself together. He told his story as simply and as calmly as he was able, detailing his mounting suspicions about Simeon's disappearance and the queen's forthcoming wedding and leaving out nothing except Joachim's use of magic, and (since Tycho was clearly beyond saving) any directly incriminating mention of Ruth, Will and Annice. It left some holes in the account, but only small ones, and he hoped the princess would not notice. As he finished, he saw that she was frowning.

'Do you believe me?' he asked unhappily.

The princess did not immediately answer. 'You have left something out,' she said, 'but nothing important, I think. Yes, Casimir, I believe you. I am just wondering what you think I can do. You see, your timing is exquisitely poor. It's Christmas Day and I have to leave Starberg within the next couple of hours. Not only that, I cannot see how I can intervene without seriously compromising my own position.'

'I thought,' said Casimir hesitantly, 'you might talk to Her Majesty.'

'Out of the question. The queen is so thoroughly under the procurator's thumb, she would go straight to him and tell him the entire story. It would be the excuse he's been waiting for ever since my return to Starberg. You forget: I gave your father the firework warrant for the wedding. Any threat of sabotage and I will take the blame. There has to be another way.' The princess appeared to consider. 'It seems to me the best thing to do is to set some men searching for your father. Discreetly. I still have my supporters in the Queen's Guard. I think something can be contrived.'

'You won't lock Simeon up, will you?' asked Casimir unhappily. 'It's not him, you know. It's Circastes who's making him behave like this.'

The princess shook her head. 'Of course I won't lock him up. That would serve no purpose at all. But you must realise, Casimir, I'll need time to do this. I will have to make some contacts—no, don't argue with me. This is too big and complicated now, I have no choice. I can't go tearing around the city like an ordinary person, and as I've said, it's Christmas. There's scarcely a person in this palace who isn't preoccupied with my sister's wretched ball.' The princess had suddenly forgotten about her journey to Osterfall, but Casimir decided it would not be politic to remind her. She stood up and rang the bell. 'Your father's shop's in Fish Lane, isn't it? Near the Cathedral? It won't be safe for you to go back there. You'd better stay here, where Greitz's leeches cannot find you. One of my men will find you a bed, since you haven't slept. And perhaps some breakfast?'

Casimir nodded. The door opened and a young man in a red-slashed uniform came into the room. He smiled slightly at Casimir's reaction and so did the princess.

'Don't worry, Casimir,' said Christina. 'There are many more men in the Queen's Guard who are loyal to me than the procurator realises. You'll be quite safe. Enjoy your breakfast and have a good rest. And thank you for coming to me. I promise, you won't regret giving me your trust.'

This time, Casimir remembered to bow. The princess smiled at him. As he left the room he noted that her feet under the expensive wrap were bare, but was too exhausted to realise what this meant.

※

Casimir's escort showed him up a tiny back staircase and delivered him to a small room with a shuttered window. It was more of a closet than anything else, its door hidden by ormolu tracings beside a fireplace. A bed had been built into the curved wall of the South Tower and furnished with clean sheets and blankets. There was a washstand with a jug and ewer, a carpet on the floor and an expensive porcelain chamberpot. All this filled the tiny space to overflowing and made it horribly claustrophobic, but Casimir's first alarmed reaction, that here was another prison, was quickly dispelled when the guard handed him the key.

'Take this,' he said. 'You can let yourself out if you have to, but it would be better if you kept the door locked. You can never predict the servants' movements, especially when it's as busy as it is today. I'll light a fire next door so you should be reasonably warm. Would you like your breakfast now?' Casimir nodded, and the man went away. He came back shortly afterwards with some tepid water for the washbasin and the promised breakfast on a tray. There was a chunk of bread, a small knobbly round of winter cheese and some underbrewed coffee without milk. Considering it was Christmas Day in a royal palace, Casimir thought they might have managed something better, but he did not think it wise to make a complaint.

He did manage to wait until the guard had left the room before he fell on the food and devoured it. The breakfast turned out to be rather better than he had expected, or perhaps it was just his hunger that made the plain bread and cheese taste so delicious. When he had finished, Casimir rinsed the worst of the vomit out of his hair, took off his boots, and climbed into bed. In the moments before he fell asleep, he remembered the story of Queen Astrid and how she had hidden her lovers in a secret room in the South Tower. Perhaps there was truth in the old stories after all.

He slept soundly until late in the afternoon. The sound of rain drumming against the window finally pulled him from a net of dreams, and he lay for a moment under the covers, recollecting where he was. Then, in the middle of the red tapestry carpet, he saw a letter, folded neatly like a child's paper boat. His first thought was that Princess Christina must have left it for him, his second, a confused realisation that he had not heard the door open, and that the key to the room was still in his pocket.

Casimir climbed out of bed and picked the letter up. The paper seemed to unfold of its own accord in his hand. There were just two words on it, in a black, familiar hand. *Wren Alley*. For a moment Casimir stared at the long-sloping *A* and wondered if there could be any mistake. Then the message faded on the page and disappeared. A faint magical scent pricked his nostrils, like the curl of smoke from an extinguished candle, and he knew he could not be wrong.

Casimir put the paper mechanically into his pocket. He pulled on his boots and buttoned his thin jacket up to the collar. Simeon needed him, and Wren Alley, wherever that was, was where he had to go. He unlocked the door of the closet and let himself out of the outer chamber. Casimir made his way downstairs into the main wing of the palace, where the preparations for the evening's celebrations were reaching a frenzied culmination. The smell of rich cakes, roast goose and other delicacies floated up from the kitchens; marble fireplaces and dozens of portable stoves were being lit to bring the huge reception rooms to an acceptable temperature before the guests arrived. In the upper galleries small orchestras were tuning strings and hautboys, and in the grand ballroom a young man with green breeches and very long legs was dancing a caper, to the immense amusement of his fellow servants. Still in his black page's uniform Casimir walked straight past them, through the door. Once outside, he crossed the River Court and passed swiftly through the sentry gate, headed for the river and Simeon's hiding place.

A mental picture flashed into his head: muddy water, a broken down warehouse, a wooden house perched on stilts like an arthritic water bird. Wren Alley was in the slums on the other side of the River Ling. Casimir turned onto King Frederik's elegant New Bridge, a royal masterpiece which contrived to be both more beautiful and less practical than the one it had replaced, and walked on briskly. On the opposite side a maze of tenements and lean-tos marked the beginning of the Watermen's Quarter, better known in Starberg as the Thieves' Margravate.

The houses were cobbled together from whatever materials were available, their walls sagged and were covered with mildew, and a foul smell rose from the pools of stagnant water which gathered between the broken cobbles. It was a fine place to avoid on a winter's evening just on nightfall, for if they even knew what it was, nobody here was likely to be celebrating Christmas. But Casimir saw no one except a ragged child and an alley cat who ran away at the sight of him. At last he found the name, Wren Alley, written in black paint on a wall near a rundown watermen's tavern. At the very end of the street, hard by a crumbling warehouse on the water's edge, was the house he was looking for.

All its windows were boarded shut and a set of steps led up to a door which hung without a landing in the middle of the wall. By now it was almost dark and bone-achingly cold; the wind blowing off the river was bitter and Casimir was wearing no topcoat, hat or gloves. He picked his way through mud and filth to climb the steps and banged on the door with his fist. After a few moments passed, Casimir knocked again. This time he heard someone moving around inside the house and, after what seemed an interminable delay, the door was cracked open by an old man with vague, rather watery brown eyes.

'Yes?'

Casimir opened his mouth. Somehow, the words he'd meant to say had disappeared and he did not know how to respond. 'Hello. I'm Casimir Runciman. Simeon's son. He sent a message for me to meet him here.'

The old man's expression was politely disinterested. 'Come in, Casimir Runciman,' he said. 'We've been expecting you. You can sit down, if you like. Your father isn't here, but we should have news of him directly.'

He stepped back and opened the door just wide enough for Casimir to squeeze through. He stood hesitantly just inside the threshold. Slowly, his eyes grew accustomed to the dimness. The old man's house was bigger than it had appeared from the street. They were standing in a large, rectangular room with a pitched roof and an upstairs gallery or sleeping loft at the opposite end; all the windows were shuttered tight against the winter cold and the only light came from a banked-down stove on the opposite wall. It was overfurnished and not even clean. The air smelled of dried herbs and urine, a trace of something very sweet, like flowers, and, overlying everything, a dead smell like a rat left forgotten in a trap. Casimir's eyes were drawn to a long, paper-strewn table in the middle of the room. Surrounded by anatomical drawings and surgical instruments, an owl lay spread-eagled in a dissecting dish.

Its legs and wings were secured by pins to the wax, its internal organs glistened in the firelight.

With its banked-down bed of coals, the stove looked more like a furnace than a domestic fireplace. A whitish vapour issued from a flask that hung tinkling over it. Somebody—a child, Casimir guessed—had been drawing on the floor in chalk and scuffed it out. Everywhere he looked there were books, immensely ancient books with their titles in foreign languages on the spine, bursting out of shelves and cupboards, lying open among the papers on the table. Bunches of dried leaves and roots hung overhead, together with other things, less readily recognisable. Casimir looked more closely and started. Hanging from the ceiling was a small stuffed crocodile, the identical twin of the one he had last seen hanging in their window.

'Come and sit down, Casimir Runciman,' said the old man again, and he pulled out a chair at the end of the table. Casimir sat down, and immediately reassuring explanations flooded his head. The chalk marks had been made by Simeon when he cast a spell to send the note to him at the palace. The crocodile *was* the one from Fish Lane; Simeon had placed a spell of recovery on it, magically calling it to him in his hiding place. As for all the books, why, they were Simeon's too, bought from second-hand bookshops in Crossgarter Row. He remembered—or did he remember? A flash of red leaped out at him from amongst the jumbled papers on the table, a firework red, instantly familiar. Casimir lifted the pages. Lying underneath, clearly marked with the Runciman label, were a roman candle, a packet of squibs, and a rocket.

'Let me get you some dinner.'

'Thank you.' Casimir waited until the old man was safely occupied at a dresser on the other side of the room, then picked up the roman candle and sniffed it. The gunpowder was fresh. According to its label it was part of a batch made in October. The squibs had been made in November, the rocket only last week. Casimir untwisted a screw of newspaper that was lying with the fireworks, tipped half a dozen small crackers out onto the table and smoothed out the wrapper. The newspaper was dated 20th December. Last Thursday. The day before the firework display at Ruth's house when Circastes had come so unexpectedly back into their lives.

Casimir put the crackers into his pocket. Something about the presence of the fireworks made him feel deeply uneasy. He could not have said exactly what it was, but perhaps it was just the fact that they were there and Simeon was not. Apart from the fireworks, Casimir could see no sign that his father had even been here, and the old man made his flesh creep for reasons even less tangible. He was still fussing around the dresser, cutting bread and pouring something dark and pungent from an ugly pewter jug. Casimir looked around the room and saw that in one corner a curtain had been drawn across as if to hide something. He stood up and quietly tiptoed across the room.

The brass rings rattled slightly against the rod as he pulled the curtain aside. Casimir paused to check the old man had not heard, then slipped behind it. He found himself in a long narrow alcove, windowless, with a black wooden floor and walls. Its low ceiling, formed in part by the floor of the sleeping area upstairs, was charted with silver constellations, but the paintwork was crudely done and the whole was blackened with years of grease and candle smoke and permeated with an unpleasant fustiness. A single candle burned with an oily smoke, dripping stalactites of tallow down its holder. Casimir examined it briefly, noting the strange smell the tallow had, but it was too deeply embedded into its holder to be taken out, and he did not like to try and shift the heavy stand. Beside it, on a lectern shaped like a pair of emaciated hands, was a squat black book with fine parchment pages. Casimir flipped over a couple of leaves, but an unpleasant sluggish electricity seemed to hang around them and the writing was a strange jumble of letters and symbols he could not understand.

He turned from the book and felt his way past a jumble of chests, a boxful of earth, an apothecary's cabinet containing who knew what medicaments. In the shadows at the other end of the alcove was a second set of curtains. They shrouded what appeared to be a couch or bed with somebody lying asleep on it, and Casimir's first response was that he had intruded into someone's bedroom. Then he realised that the sleeper's posture was unnaturally still.

'Simeon?' The sleeping figure was small, too small, he hoped, to be his father, though it was hard to be sure. Quietly, Casimir approached the curtain and drew it back. A pall made of some dark, shiny material lay draped over the bed; the curtain fabric caught its folds as he pulled it back, and it began sliding inexorably towards him. Casimir grabbed at it. The material slipped through his fingers and then he saw what was lying underneath and the covers fell unnoticed to the floor.

Lying on the bed was a dead woman, a stranger, in a faded green dress. Casimir did not think she had been dead very long, though in this cold weather it was possible he was wrong. Her face was so knocked about, so broken by cuts and bruises it was hard to tell her age or what she had looked like in life, though her dress had a girl's cut about it. Her left hand had been cut off and sat like a dead spider curled up on her breast. A little blood seeped waterily from the jagged flesh and the open eyes which stared up at him were as glazed and flat as those of a fish.

A door clicked open in Casimir's head as the spell that had been controlling his thoughts suddenly broke. All the smells he had been struggling to identify resolved in a rush: death, decay and above all, magic. The corpse continued to stare at him, the expression in its eyes neither peaceful nor even horrified, but simply empty. Casimir backed away, turned and ran. At the end of the alcove he slammed into the old man with his blank, baby face, the pewter jug in his hand and bread crumbs on his lips.

Casimir floundered, tangled in material. With a great ripping sound the curtain tore loose from its rings. The old man looked at him with interest. He put down his jug and pinched out the candle, then turned his eyes to the bed.

'I fished her out of the pool at the bottom of the waterfall,' he said. 'You can always pick the suicides.

The murder victims, they're weighed down with bricks or stones, but the suicides float and bang against the rocks. Do you think Peter and Christina will be pleased?'

Casimir flung off the curtain and ran for the door. The bolts tugged at his fingertips, the door banged open against the wall. He was standing in the doorway, hanging on the brink of nothing. The steps into Wren Alley had disappeared. Mist swirled patchily, but it was not river mist. The door had opened onto a sheer fall of mountainous rock.

Water roared somewhere close by and the air was deathly cold. A bird cawed in the distance. Casimir turned back to the old man. 'What is this place? Where have you brought me?'

'Why, to our house in Outer Osterfall, of course,' said the old man. 'You're here to be apprenticed to my son. Simeon's boy, the one Peter's waited for all these years. He's with your father now, in the cellar with the fireworks and when they're done, my little Christina will be queen. Please come away from the door, Casimir Runciman. It's a long way down and the rocks are dangerous if you fall.'

Casimir moved away from the door. 'What do you mean? What's my father to you?'

'I'm Ezekial Circastes,' said the old man simply. 'Your father Simeon was my apprentice.'

'Your apprentice?'

Casimir stopped. For the first time he looked at the old man with eyes undeceived by magic. Ezekial had picked up the torn curtain and was rethreading the hooks; his face sagged in pouches like a baby's, but the underlying bone structure was there. He resembled his son—or rather, Circastes resembled his father—in the same way the crayon portrait of Princess Christina's dark-haired aunt had reminded him of Circastes. Which meant Christina. . .

The princess herself had been here, in this house, this afternoon. Now that Casimir had made the connection, the scent of her floral perfume lingered, so distinct and strong it could almost mask the scent of her magic. She had tricked him, lured him here into a trap of her family's making. Meanwhile Simeon and Circastes were holed up in the treasurer's cellar with the complete contents of the firework shop. Casimir knew what that meant. Some time tonight, during the queen's Christmas ball when the entire court was assembled, Simeon was going to blow up the palace and himself with it. Princess Christina, miraculously called out of Starberg, would survive to become Queen of Ostermark and Casimir would become the magician's apprentice in Simeon's place. He remembered what Simeon had told him: how on the day he had been apprenticed, all his memories had been wiped from his head. Soon, all Casimir was and all he had been, all his memories of his parents, all the brave and funny and wonderful and beautiful and frightening moments of his life would be taken away from him. Casimir Runciman, the firework maker's apprentice, would cease to exist, and then the cycle of Circastes's revenge would be complete.

Casimir felt himself flooded by an anguish so acute it was physical. Ezekial looked up. For a moment his mad face seemed to soften in sympathy.

'Don't worry, firework boy,' he said. 'Peter knows what he's doing. Everything will be all right.'

'No, it won't!' cried Casimir. 'How can it be all right when my father is going to die? And what about me? Don't I have a right to be who I am, to die the same person I was born?'

'Simeon has to be punished,' said Ezekial. 'Peter says he must.'

'But he *has* been punished,' said Casimir passionately. 'All these years he's been punished. He's never forgiven himself for what he did. He was only seventeen. He didn't know what he was doing.'

Ezekial shook his head. 'You're wrong.' He finished re-hanging the curtain and fetched the candle from the alcove. 'Your father did know. A magician must never force control on another magician. That is the one rule we all follow. I know what Simeon did to me and why. Paulina and Peter were able to bring some things back. But your father was incompetent. He botched the spell and it couldn't be reversed.' He set down the candle and began retracing some of the chalk outlines on the floor. Casimir watched apprehensively, but the old man had apparently lost interest in talking to him. He produced a dish of what looked like dried mud and scattered it in the circle. Then he lit a long spill at the furnace and touched it to the candle.

Suddenly Casimir realised what he was doing. The chalk circle, the candle, the mud from the river at Wren Alley: the old man was re-opening the way to Starberg. Someone—Christina, her aunt, Circastes—was coming through. The fog in the doorway shimmered and the sound of roaring water was replaced by the river splashing against the pylons of the house in Wren Alley. Casimir started inching towards the door.

Ezekial blew out the spill and looked up.

'No!' he said, and came swiftly between Casimir and the door. Casimir backed off. He put his hand into his pocket and felt his fist close unexpectedly around the string of crackers he had put there earlier.

'What are you doing?'

'Nothing.' Casimir took his hand out of his pocket and inched away from the door. The furnace was behind him now, so close that the heat from the exposed coals burned the backs of his legs through his breeches. He put his hand behind his back. There was a moment of agony as his fingers burned, then the fuse sizzed and he flung up his arm.

'Look out!'

Ezekial turned. Casimir hurled the crackers straight at him. The old man screamed, half-dived, half-tripped and fell to the floor and then the fireworks went off with a string of rapid explosions, like corks popping out of a bottle.

Casimir pelted across the room and hurled himself through the door. The stairs seemed to dissolve underneath him and he lost his footing. He had a brief, swift impression of wooden beams and props flying past and then he hit the soft mud below with a thudding splat.

For a moment he sat, unable to do more than catch his breath. Wren Alley buzzed around him. Then a voice spoke loudly, making him jump.

'My God,' it said. 'What an entrance. What the hell do you think you're doing?'

A man in a uniform was standing a few feet away, a lantern in his hand. Casimir opened his mouth to shout for help, then saw that it was Joachim.

'What am I doing? What are *you* doing here?'

'What do you think, you blue-arsed fool?' His uncle reached out a hand and hauled him up out of the mud. 'I've been looking for you since daybreak. Are you out of your mind, coming on your own to a place like this?'

'I've been looking for Simeon.' Casimir suddenly remembered. 'He sent me a letter. Only it was a trap. It was Circastes and he's with Simeon now, in the cellar under the palace!'

'Circastes?'

'Yes.' Casimir shivered, and Joachim pulled off his topcoat.

'Here, put this on. You can explain about it later, I've got a boat waiting over here.' He led the way across the mud flats to a small, flat-bottomed skiff. Casimir climbed in and unshipped the oars. As Joachim untied it from its mooring and pushed it out into deeper water, a thought occurred to him.

'Is this boat yours?'

Joachim's teeth flashed white in the dirty, rain-smudged shadow of his face. 'What do you think?' He scrambled over the side, and for a moment the boat rocked wildly. Then the current caught and whisked them away downstream, and Wren Alley receded into rain and darkness.

CHAPTER ELEVEN

'I suppose I ought to warn you I killed a man,' said Joachim as they skimmed along. Casimir looked alarmed. His uncle went on, 'That was how I knew where to look for you. When I got out of the Undercroft, I went straight to the firework shop. I found a little leech belonging to the princess. He told me to go to Wren Alley and was kind enough to lend me his uniform before he died. Just so you know you're associating with a desperate criminal who might be arrested at any moment.'

'How did you get out of the Undercroft?' asked Casimir.

'I escaped. Do you want the long version, or the simple one? The simple one, I think. I won't go into the unpleasant details of my arrest. Suffice it to say that I was knocked out like a fool from behind and unconscious for a lot of it. When I finally came to my senses I was in the Undercroft, and there on the floor of my cell was that prize idiot, Marcus Tycho. I don't know what they'd done to him, but he was in pretty bad shape. He died soon after midnight and the guards came and stitched him up in a sack with some lead weights. When they were out of the room—I suppose they thought I was still *non compos mentis*—I pulled the weights out and propped the body up against the wall. We're about the same build and colouring and when I dressed him in my shirt and trousers, it looked just like me, asleep. Then I got into the sack and closed it with a knot I could undo from the inside and they sent me down the chute into the Ling. Interesting. I was never quite sure whether the famous chute really existed. It was quite an education to find it did.'

'I was arrested, too,' said Casimir. 'I think they were hoping I'd lead them to Simeon. They questioned me and let me go this morning.'

'That'll be something to impress your girlfriends with,' said Joachim. 'It's certainly an impressive bump you've got on your head.'

'It still aches.'

'I bet it does. I've a little experience of these things myself.'

'There's something else you need to know,' said Casimir. 'The procurator suspects Princess Christina. He thinks she's a magician and he's right. She's Circastes's niece. That's why Circastes has Simeon and all the fireworks and gunpowder in the treasurer's cellar. He's going to get him to blow up the palace so Christina can become queen.'

'Christina's a magician, too? Well, that's not surprising. There was certainly talk about her mother, years ago. She came to court as the mistress of some tinpot local nobleman and was supposed to have bewitched the king. Of course, people tend to underestimate the depths of inanity males descend to in the grip of lust. Here, give me the oars, you're getting tired.' They changed places and Joachim started cutting more swiftly across the current, steering for the southern arches of the bridge. 'Now I come to think on it, I seem to remember Simeon telling me there was a much older sister. She was the eldest, I think she ran off with a man. They were never allowed to mention her name. Of course, it all happened before his time. The one he used to talk about was called Paula, something like that.'

'Paulina. She was the aunt who brought Christina up. She told me she was dying and she had to go to her.'

'Well, naturally. Christina's got to have an excuse not to be in the palace when it explodes. And you can bet Paulina will have been in this up to her eyeballs from the beginning. She's got more grudges against your father than anyone.'

'What do you mean?'

'Don't you know? That's what the original spell was. The one Simeon cast that caused all the trouble. He and Circastes were about the same age, but Paulina was a few years older, twenty-one or so. Simeon rather fancied her, but she had bigger fish to fry. He tried to cast a glamour out of one of the grimoires to make himself look older, so she would pay him some attention.' Joachim showed his teeth. 'Believe it or not, that's what all this is about. An adolescent love charm that went wrong.'

'Don't tell me: I don't want to know.' Sickened, Casimir turned away and hunched over, staring at the river. Ahead of them oil lamps gleamed on King Frederik's new bridge, one for every narrow pointed arch. Joachim manoeuvred the boat expertly. As they approached the dark tunnel of the second arch the current gathered speed and shot them through, swirling them down two or three heartstopping feet into the lower reaches near the River Court.

The river flowed on, a pockmarked ribbon, its murky grey indistinguishable from sky or shore. Joachim steered their boat in amongst the wherries and disused summer pleasure barges and tied it up to an unobtrusive mooring. In the River Court footmen hurried through puddles with umbrellas and the coaches jostled for position as one by one they rolled up and disgorged their occupants, great men dressed in lace and velvet and scented elegant ladies. Nobody bothered to look at a member of the Queen's Guard in a too-small uniform and a page in filthy livery as they ran up the steps of the treasurer's darkened house and banged on his front door.

Their knock was answered by a very junior footman. 'May I help you?'

Casimir pushed past him into the house.

'Ruth!' he yelled. 'Ruth, where are you?'

Ruth appeared on the landing at the top of the stairs. She was wearing an old dress and felt slippers and her hair was dishevelled. Her little dog darted out from under her skirts and started barking.

'Casimir! What do you want? Where's Simeon?'

'He's here.'

'What do you mean, he's here?' Ruth came downstairs, her dog running ahead and yapping around their ankles. The footman withdrew at her approach and she rounded on Casimir. 'Casimir, what are you talking about? I warn you, if this is another of your—'

'Never mind all this,' interrupted Joachim. 'We haven't got time. Quickly. Did Simeon have a key to the cellar?'

'What do you mean?'

'Could Simeon have access to the cellar without your knowledge?'

'What cellar?'

'Stop prevaricating!' shouted Joachim. Ruth appeared startled and backed off a little.

'He didn't have a key,' she said, 'if that's what you're asking. But I have keys to all the locks in this house and he knew where I kept them, so if I wasn't here and he wanted to get in, I suppose he could. He wouldn't have done it without my permission, though. Simeon's not that sort of person.'

'Well, he's down there now,' said Joachim. 'Are you going to tell me he asked your permission before he filled your cellars with gunpowder?'

'Fireworks, yes—'

'Gunpowder, fireworks, it's all the same,' said Joachim. 'I tell you, Simeon is down there now with enough explosives to blow up this house, the palace and half the River Court down to the Undercroft. Circastes has him in thrall. So has that sly-faced bitch Christina. Now get your keys, and get down there fast, or none of us are going to be around long enough to argue!'

'Christina?' Ruth started fumbling in her pocket. Casimir broke away and ran down the corridor to the servants' stairs. The sound of Christmas festivities and drunken laughter floated out to him from the staff dining hall, and the carriageway at the back of the house was jammed with coaches, drivers, grooms, stablehands all shouting and trying to find places to park. Casimir darted out between the coaches and hurried down the stairs to the cellar.

'Simeon!' he yelled. 'Simeon, Simeon!' He banged on the door, but there was no answer. A moment later, Joachim and Ruth appeared behind him with a lantern, Ruth carrying a huge bunch of keys.

'What's in there?' Joachim indicated the door.

'The mortars from the ordnance. Fireworks. I let Simeon put them there. His powder cellar was full.'

'Not any more,' said Casimir. 'He's taken everything out of it and the shop, too. Even the firework boy.'

Ruth rattled her fingers through the bunch of keys. 'My key's gone. Someone's taken it.'

'Then we'll pick the lock.' Joachim brought a loop of wire out of his pocket. Ruth shook her head.

'That's no use. There are bolts and a bar on the other side. Simeon and I used to meet in there at one time when we wanted to be private.' She bent and peered through the keyhole. 'Simeon? Simeon, are you there?'

There was no reply. Ruth banged on the door. 'Simeon? Simeon, let me in!'

'Get a crowbar,' said Joachim. 'We'll have to break it down.'

'No!' said Ruth. 'There are too many people out in the carriageway, someone might hear.'

'I don't give a damn about people hearing.' Joachim picked up a coal shovel which was standing against the wall and smashed it against the lock. The wood splintered and the door gave perhaps an inch. Casimir peered through the gap.

'Careful! He's got barrels of gunpowder stacked up against it!'

Joachim pushed him out of the way and applied his own eye to the gap. 'You're right. The door opens inwards, we'll never get it open from this side. Is there any other way in?'

'No,' said Ruth.

'Yes, there is,' said Casimir. 'There's another door. I found it the other day when I was looking over the mortars. It's on the bottom wall, the one nearest the river.'

'That's not a door,' objected Ruth. 'It's an inspection hatch. There's a passage that goes down to the river near the water wheel. You can't get in at the other end, the entrance is underwater.'

Casimir took a deep breath. 'I can swim.'

'Swim!' Ruth exclaimed, and then stopped. She and Joachim exchanged glances.

Joachim shrugged. 'He might be able to do it. Do you have any idea how far down the entrance is?'

'Fifteen feet, perhaps. I've only seen it drained once and that was years ago.' Ruth turned to Casimir. 'Cas, it's not just a matter of swimming. You'd have to dive, really dive, and find your way down by touch. Do you honestly think you can do it?'

'Yes,' said Casimir, with more certainty than he felt. He had learned to swim years before, following the far off summer when he had nearly drowned in the upper reaches of the Ling. After he'd hauled him out, Simeon had spent several months teaching him every time they came near water. In the end, he'd become quite good. It was a long time since he had practised, but he had been told that the skill was never forgotten.

It was good enough for Joachim. 'We'll give it a try, then. Ruth, you know the way. You'll have to take him.'

'All right,' said Ruth. 'I'm still technically under house arrest, but my father bribed them to call the guard off and he's the only one who'd bother to stop me. Cas, I'll have to get a rope. I'll meet you in the hall in two minutes.'

She turned and ran up the stairs. Casimir started to follow, but Joachim grabbed him by the shoulder.

'Casimir,' he said, 'listen. This is dangerous. Circastes may still be in there. At the very least, he'll be watching. If you get through to the cellar, be very careful. Try and talk some sense into Simeon if it seems appropriate. Otherwise, try and move the barrels away from the door. I'll be here on the other side. If there's any way humanly possible for me to get in, I'll do it.'

'All right,' said Casimir, though he did not like his uncle's use of the word 'if'.

'Good lad,' said Joachim. He squeezed Casimir's shoulder and gave him a little push towards the stairs.

'Good luck.'

Casimir retraced his steps to the house. He found Ruth waiting in the hall as promised. She had changed her slippers for thick leather boots and was wearing a drab, heavy coat over her house dress. A coil of rope was slung over her shoulder.

'Are you ready? Casimir, I hope you know what you're doing.'

Ruth opened the front door and pushed him out into the rain. Next door, the palace was lit up like a display of fireworks, its black and yellow flags hanging waterlogged in the rain. Strains of music floated out and were damped by the continuing downpour; there were guards on sentry duty, but the worst of the traffic had cleared. The line of street lamps along the carriageway cast yellow reflections in the puddles. Ruth crossed the River Court and hurried down the water stairs. She was surprisingly fleet-footed and Casimir had to run to keep up with her.

'Where is it?' he panted.

'Over there.' Ruth pointed upriver. 'See the water wheel under the bridge, between the first and second piers? The entrance is next to the first pier, the one on the embankment. Follow me and I'll show you.'

She climbed over the stone balustrade and jumped down onto the river embankment. Casimir followed her. Ahead of them, the water wheel streamed black with water, invested with a clanking life of its own. It supplied the palace and all the buildings along the River Court with running water, and was a favourite spot for suicides, since the wheel generally finished those who thought twice and tried to swim. Ruth picked her way over broken stonework into the shadow of the bridge. She turned and took the lantern from Casimir and shone it into a gap in the masonry.

'There it is.' She had to shout to make herself heard over the deafening clatter of the turning wheel. 'It was built when they laid out the River Court. They still use it from time to time—in spring the cellars can fill up with water and they use it to pump them out.'

Casimir followed the beam of light. Hard by the first pier and covered with a grating was a deep, dark well, perhaps three feet across and filled with dirty-looking water. At the sight of it, his heart sank. Had their situation been less desperate he would have given up there and then, but Ruth had already set down the lantern and her rope and was struggling with the grating. Casimir went to help her. The grating came away more easily than he had expected, but if anything, the well looked even more intimidating uncovered.

Ruth uncoiled the rope and tied one end around her waist. For want of something better to do, Casimir took off Joachim's topcoat and his boots and stockings. A fine spume hung in the air from the water wheel; it was deathly cold and settled in droplets on his skin. His bare feet slithered on the stonework. Ruth put her hand into an inner pocket and handed him a key.

'Take off your coat and jacket.' Ruth watched while he buttoned the key into his breeches' pocket. 'Can you do a running knot? Good. Loop this rope around your waist—that's it, not too tight. When you're safely through to the passage, jerk the rope twice. If you get into trouble, jerk it three times and I'll try and haul you back. It's not quite low tide, so the opening shouldn't be more than about twelve feet down on the pier side of the shaft. Do you understand?'

Casimir nodded, almost deafened by the rattle of the wheel. The water in the well was very black and its surface crawled with vibration. He sat down and dangled his feet over the edge. Then, not wishing to prolong his misery, he slipped in with a splash and a yelp of shock.

'It's *freezing*!'

'Don't waste time,' said Ruth. 'In this cold you'll only have a few minutes before your muscles cramp. The sooner you find the opening, the sooner you can get out.'

The fact that she was right didn't make Casimir like her any the better for it. The water was so cold it hurt. He flipped head over heels and thrust off against the brickwork, trying to stay on the vertical as he dived down the shaft, but instead slamming almost immediately into the side. Casimir floundered, losing his bearings and most of his breath. He returned to the surface, gasped another lungful of wintry air and, with a renewed sense of the difficulties confronting him, tried again.

The second dive was slightly more successful. This time, he splayed out his hands to touch the walls as he went down, and it was easier, though the sensation of going down through the thick black water was curiously unpleasant, as if he were a pen being plunged into an inkwell. The machinery reverberated in the enclosed space, setting up an unbearable pressure in his ears; this, and the numbing pain of simply being in the water blotted out almost all other sensation. Casimir had no idea how deep he had dived, but after several seconds he felt the blood pounding in his temples and realised he was starting to tire. For a few more seconds he struggled to go deeper, but there was no sign of any opening, and as his lungs strained with the effort of holding in his breath, he was gripped by a horrible vision of being stuck in the shaft and drowning upside down. With difficulty Casimir turned and struck upwards in a flurry of bubbles. His head broke through the surface of the water and the cold air slammed against his face.

'No luck?' shouted Ruth, over the noise of the machinery.

'No.'

'Try again.'

On the third attempt, just before his air ran out, he found it.

The opening was reasonably large, about the size of a small window, which he supposed for an inspection hatch was about right. Casimir tried to feel his way into the passage, but his hands encountered an unexpected obstruction. He ran his fingers carefully over it. A moment later his air ran out and he had to return to the surface.

'What's the matter?' shouted Ruth when she saw him.

'There's bars on it! I can't get through!'

'Bars?'

'There's two of them. About an inch thick. I think it must be some sort of grating.'

'Try and move it.'

'I can't.' The thought of going back down the dark, freezing shaft and drowning, caught on the grating without any chance of escape, filled Casimir with terror.

'It's set into the stone and there's a padlock. I'll never be able to shift it.'

'Then try the key. Or wriggle through the gap. If there's only two bars there must be an opening in the middle of at least a foot. You're not so big you can't get through that. You have to try, Casimir. We've come this far. You've got to make the effort!'

'I can't! I'm too big. If I get stuck, I'll drown, and who's going to rescue me then?' Casimir tried to hoist himself out of the water. Ruth grabbed hold of his shirt. For a moment they struggled on the edge of the shaft and then she pushed him back in so hard he knocked his elbow agonisingly on the stonework.

'You coward! Get back down there! Your father's about to kill himself and all you care about is yourself!'

'That's not true! Why don't you do it, if you're so brave?'

'Because I can't swim! If I could, I would. It's like everything else, Casimir. Something goes wrong and you automatically blame me. Well, this time it's not my fault. You thought of it, you damn well do it!'

Black rage swelled up in Casimir. 'God, I *hate* you,' he shouted. 'You're a miserable bitch. I hate you more than anybody else in the entire world. I wish my father had never *met* you.'

'And I wish I'd never met you. If you don't go back down the shaft, Simeon will die. He's your father, doesn't that mean anything?'

'Die? We're all going to die, anyway. When that cellar explodes it will take out the entire River Court—' Casimir stopped. How could he explain to her that there *was* a difference? All his life, he had lived with the dread of being caught in an explosion, but it was a fear he had come to terms with. It wasn't the same as drowning helplessly, upside down, like a kitten in a bucket of water. And if he did get through, if he did find Simeon, what could he hope to achieve? With a sudden fatalistic clarity, Casimir realised that, whatever he did now, Simeon was going to die, that the dark tapestry of his father's life had unravelled beyond hope of repair. Simeon's story was like a firework display on the blackest of nights, the darkness punctuated with flashes of coruscating brilliance. Then, as soon as they had been glimpsed, they vanished, leaving only the rumbling aftershocks of the explosions, the shower of ash, the stench of gunpowder hanging in the rain.

And now it had come down to this: two sodden figures, glaring at each other across a filthy puddle of water. In Simeon's life, Casimir knew there had been so few flashes of light that it would be callous of him not to admit Ruth had been one of them. Yet he did not know what to say to her: this angry, difficult woman, who lacked all gentleness and tolerance, whom he disliked so much and yet, whom his father had loved. She had not answered his outburst, but her face was working now in the lamplight, a mix of anger, dislike, distress. Then he realised that the wetness on her cheeks was not raindrops, but tears. The unexpected weakness threw him off his guard.

'I'm sorry,' he said. 'I didn't mean it. I don't hate you, really. I just said it to upset you.'

'I know,' said Ruth. 'I'm not crying because of what you said, Casimir. God knows, I've been called worse, more times than I can remember. No. If I'm crying, I suppose it's because of all the might-have-beens. My life's been full of them. I suppose this is just another.' She looked away. 'When I was your age I desperately didn't want to die, either. I almost did. I had a baby and it nearly killed me. In the years since then, I've often wished it had. If he'd lived, my son would have been about the same age as you.'

Casimir clung to the side of the shaft. The pain from the cold had subsided to a sinister ache and he could no longer feel his fingers where they gripped the stonework. He knew he was slowly freezing, being overcome by the icy water, but in the scheme of things it hardly seemed to matter. Ruth picked up the rope and started pulling it out of the water. Impulsively, Casimir shot out a hand and grabbed it.

'Wait,' he said. 'Once more. I'll try once more.' Ruth started to protest, but Casimir knew that if he got out now, he would never get back in. He flipped backwards quickly, down into the water. This time, knowing where it was, he was able to dive straight to the opening.

Casimir grasped the iron bars and pushed his head into the gap. It was, as Ruth had said, wider than he had initially thought, and though it would easily have stopped a grown man, or even a youth less wiry than himself, there was plenty of space for him to wriggle into. If he had been able to see it would have been comparatively easy; as it was, the darkness terrified as much as it thwarted him. Casimir's shoulders jammed and his legs caught against the wall of the shaft. A few bubbles escaped from the sides of his mouth. It's your fault, Ruth, if I drown, he thought, and then like a miracle his shoulders scraped in the opening and he was through.

Casimir kicked out and started swimming as fast as he could. His head pounded from the effort of keeping the air in his lungs and his eyes flashed red. Bubbles burst from his mouth, and then he suddenly realised he was going upward, that he was trying to swim in shallow water, and that there was a gap between the water and the ceiling of the passage.

'Thank God!' Casimir's head burst through the surface and he flopped over onto his back and floated, breathing in great rasping lungfuls of dank air. A dizzying sense of thankfulness flooded through his body. Then he tried to stand up. Immediately his legs gave way and he fell over. The effort of the swim had left him spent.

The rope was still tied to his waist, and, remembering Ruth, he gave it two shaky tugs. They were answered by a sharp jerk at the other end, then the rope went slack. Casimir untied it and dropped it into the water. This time, when he tried to stand up, he was able to stagger a few steps before he fell. The water grew shallower and shallower and at last he splashed into a passage. Casimir waited a few moments longer to recover his breath, then started feeling his way along the passage wall.

His clothes were heavy with water and he was deathly cold, but the passage was not as long as he had expected it to be. After a few minutes of fumbling his way in the darkness he found it starting to slope upwards, and then his hands encountered a door. There was no handle on it, just a keyhole. Casimir inserted the key Ruth had given him into the lock and turned it. The door was swollen and took several shoves before it gave so much as a finger-width; when it did open, the hinges were so stiff with rust they squealed like a churchyard gate. But for all the effect the noise had, Casimir might have saved himself the effort of trying to be quiet. He was in the right place, but nothing else in the cellar was as he'd expected.

An orange light burned dimly in the middle of the room. Casimir could see a human figure hunched over it, so motionless it might have been a statue. Around the perimeter he could make out the shadowy outlines of powder barrels and firework boxes, the open mouths of the ordnance mortars arranged in an inward-pointing circle. Casimir took a step into the room. A box of fireworks thudded onto the floor from a precariously stacked bundle at his elbow; he jumped, but no one else stirred, and after a moment his fright abated enough for him to take a few more cautious steps forward.

The floor was scattered with cracked and broken firework cases and felt gritty under his bare feet. Gunpowder had been strewn in deliberately regular patterns, spiralling out like a maze or mosaic from the light in the middle of the room; each trail divided, and divided again until there were dozens ringing the cellar in concentric circles. Around the walls these powder trails terminated in well-caulked kegs of gunpowder, boxes of fireworks, and fuses leading to the ordnance mortars, which had evidently been cleaned and loaded.

Half a dozen powder kegs were stacked in front of the main door. In the middle of the room, huddled over a firepot with his face surrounded by a halo of tiny lights, sat Simeon.

'Father?'

Trembling, Casimir knelt and took his hand. It lay limply in his own; when he shook Simeon's shoulder and touched his face, he did not even respond. Pieces of lighted slow match were knotted in his hair, burning like fireflies with a mingled smell of gunpowder and singed hair. His eyes were vague and without recognition. Intellectually, Casimir had known to expect something of the sort. Nevertheless, he had not expected the expression on Simeon's face to look so disturbingly like Ezekial Circastes's when he had opened the door to him in Wren Alley.

A single spark would be enough to set off the contents of the cellar. Casimir remembered what Joachim had said about moving matches and tinder from Simeon's reach, and started inching the firepot away from him, carefully, for the pottery was burning hot and there were no pot tongs. Instantly, Simeon's hand flashed out and grabbed his wrist.

'Ow! Let go!' Casimir tried to wrest himself free, but Simeon's grip only tightened. With inhuman strength he started forcing Casimir's hand up and back from the firepot, until Casimir felt as if every bone in his arm was about to break. Outside in the stairwell someone started banging on the door. Casimir heard Joachim's voice calling out to him, demanding to know if he was there, and then the air moved silently behind and around him.

A human hand came down briefly on his shoulder and a quiet voice said, 'Stop.'

At once, the dreadful pressure on Casimir's wrist released. Wrung white, it dropped lifelessly to his lap. The hand lifted from his shoulder and a slight figure circled around between him and Simeon. All the hairs stood up on the back of Casimir's neck as if a ghost had entered the room. But Circastes did not even look at him. Instead he sat down and gently took Simeon's hand. Simeon whimpered, and, like a child, he laid his head on Circastes's shoulder.

The magician put his arms around him and drew him close. With great care, he brushed the burning pieces of slow match away from Simeon's cheeks and started speaking in a language Casimir could not understand. The words were all elegant sibilances and rolling vowels, strung together with a cadence he had never heard in all his wide travels in Ostermark, not even among the sailors of every nation whom he had encountered in the great ports on the North Sea. Yet Simeon clearly understood, for from time to time he interjected in the same language, his voice so forlorn it pierced Casimir's heart to hear it. He was listening to the language of his father's childhood, the source of the accent that had always marked Simeon out as a foreigner though he claimed no country of his own, the source too, of the even slighter inflection, no more than an occasional catch, in Casimir's own speech. He did not know what the two men were talking about, but he could guess, for tears were slowly coursing down his father's cheeks. Then he saw that Circastes was crying, too. The magician's face was grey and ravaged by fatigue and a dozen mingled emotions, too raw to be anything but genuine.

'Stop it,' said Casimir helplessly. 'Please. Stop it.' As he spoke, he realised what a ridiculous thing it was to have said, for clearly Simeon did not even recognise he was there. But though his father's expression did not change, Peter Circastes stopped his murmuring. With his arm still around Simeon's shoulders, he turned and looked at Casimir.

'If this could have been stopped, Cas, believe me, I would have done it twenty years ago. I'm not here because I want to be.'

'No,' said Casimir. 'You're the one who had the choice in this. You made this happen. You forced Simeon to come here. And you knew I would come, too, because he's my father. Because I wanted—'

'To say goodbye.'

'Yes.'

'Because you parted on bad terms.'

'Yes.'

'And because you love him. Most of all, you came because of that.' Circastes paused. 'In which case, you'll understand why I'm here, too. And why I, equally, have no choice in the matter.'

The comparison silenced him. Outmanoeuvred, Casimir groped for an appropriate response and found none. He had expected some mummer's devil in a black suit, streaking fire and pyrotechnic flames, not this quiet man with his gentle manner and dark curls, and the sad, compelling eyes. Circastes made him feel as if

190

there was nothing he could say, and probably, there wasn't. The magician knew him too well. For the past three days he had had free access to every thought inside his head, shaping his hopes and his fears, and all this time he had been seeking out the heart of him, like water finding its level. Then he and Christina had used this knowledge to push Casimir and Simeon inexorably apart, even to this reckoning in the darkness. It was easy to be frightened of Circastes, but not so easy to hate him. Hate was not a complicated enough word to describe how Casimir felt.

'Cas.'

'Don't call me Cas.'

'Casimir, then. I don't expect you to understand why I'm doing this. All I want you to believe is that I take no pleasure in it. I'm not a monster. Whatever garbled stories Simeon has told you, this is not about revenge. It is punishment.'

'This business has wrecked my father's life,' said Casimir. 'Simeon's punished himself every day, for the last twenty years. What more do you hope to win by doing this?'

'You,' said Circastes simply. 'Because you're the one I've always really wanted. Ever since you were a tiny boy and I found out that you existed, in that mining camp at the back of Skelling. Your uncle didn't tell you the entire truth about that, Casimir. It's true, I did befriend your mother, and I turned her on your father. But it wasn't Joachim who stopped me. It was you. You came out from behind a curtain and started punching and kicking me in the back of the legs. I could have killed you then, or taken you with me, but I didn't. You were too young, only six or seven. Instead I made Simeon promise to give you over to me, when you were old enough. I didn't expect him to keep his promise, but I fully intend to hold him to it.'

'I don't believe you.'

'You mean, you don't want to. Nevertheless, it's true. Think back over the last few days, Casimir. I came to the shop in a boy's shape without your even knowing who I was. You asked me in, we talked together, I could have done whatever I wanted to you at any time since then. Yet, I never harmed you, and when the Queen's Guard came, I saved your life. Look at the scar on your chest and tell me I'm lying.'

'You tried to kill me in the park.'

'No. I forced Simeon to stop pretending and admit what he was. And what you can be. If he had given you to me then, when I asked him, it would have stopped there. We could have found another way of doing what Christina wanted. But your father refused. He's not an honourable man, Casimir. Any promise he's ever made me, he's reneged on. Let me tell you what I found when I came home, that night, twenty years ago. I found my elderly father, lying on the floor in the dark. As far as I could make out, he had been there for three days, exactly where Simeon had left him. The door was open, the fire had gone out, he could not walk or even get up off the floor, and he was almost dead from dehydration and cold. It was as if someone had abandoned a newborn baby. That is what your father did to mine, Casimir. It was not enough for him simply to destroy my father's mind. He left him to die as well.'

'If my father was so dishonourable,' said Casimir softly, 'I wonder why it is you would want me.'

He lifted his eyes. Across the cellar where the firework boxes were piled three deep against the wall the firework boy stood, face out in a jumble of dismantled set pieces, regarding him through catherine wheel eyes. The memory of the inconsequential pride he had once felt in what was now, in the scheme of things, such an insignificant achievement, made something ache in Casimir's marrow. In five short days his life had been so completely changed he could scarcely remember how the person who had set off for the firework display had felt. Even if he escaped Circastes and got out of the cellar alive, he could not go back now. Too much had happened to him, and too many people had died that he might live. His future had been too dearly bought, with blood and fire, for it to be ever entirely his own again.

'All right,' he said. 'What do you want of me?'

Circastes had his answer ready. 'I want you to give me the power of your name. And I want you to come with me. Willingly. Not because I force you to by magic or other means, but because you acknowledge that it is right.'

'And if I can't do that?'

'Then you are free to go. But your father stays. Here, in this cellar, right until the end, with his memory and understanding restored him. In the full knowledge of what he has done and why he is here.'

'Fair enough. But what about the people in the palace?'

'You're worried about them? I'm afraid there is nothing I can change, there. That is our commitment to

Christina, it cannot be broken. But I will be frank, Casimir: as far as my family is concerned, your acquiescence will wipe out Simeon's debt. If you agree to come with me, if you give me the power of your name, I promise, Simeon will be sent away safely—say, to somewhere where his skills with gunpowder would come in useful. In fact, with my niece's permission, he could even become a Captain of the Ordnance here in Starberg, with a view to rapid promotion. To have one of our own kind in such a position would have distinct advantages.'

'Simeon won't agree to that,' said Casimir flatly. 'You're wasting your time if you think he will.'

'We'd have to ensure his loyalty, of course.'

'Yes. And that's the problem, isn't it? Ensuring loyalties. If I come with you, I need to know I'm making my own mind up. Under the circumstances it's a bit hard to be sure of that.' Casimir felt tired. 'I don't want to come with you. I don't want to be a magician. It's never brought my father any joy, and I don't imagine it will bring me any, either. But I'll agree to what you suggest, on two conditions. The first is, that you don't take away my memories. I want to remember my father and who I am. The second—' he broke off, gathering the strength to say it, '—the second, is that you make sure Simeon doesn't remember anything about me.'

'That would defeat the purpose of what we're doing,' said Circastes softly.

'That's too bad, then.' Casimir stood up, stiffly, and brushed the gunpowder off his clothes. He could hear voices talking, very faintly, somewhere in the background, but could not make out where exactly they were coming from. 'Because it's the only way I'll come with you. Unless you choose to take me along by force. Chances are you'll do that, anyway, but I think that would defeat your purposes as well.'

'Wait.' Circastes stood up, too. A fist banged on the main door. Then Ruth's voice called out, unmistakably, from the stairwell outside.

'Casimir! Casimir, it's Ruth. Can you hear me? Are you there? What's happening?'

'Don't answer her.' Circastes looked at Simeon, and a strange expression passed over his face. 'All right Casimir. I agree to your conditions. If you mean what you say, give me the power of your name, now. All you have to do is say it.'

Casimir drew a deep breath. 'I, Casimir Runciman, give you the power of my name.'

As the words left his lips, there was a sharp crack and a sound of splintering wood. A small keg of slow composition fell from the stack in front of the main door. Its lid came off and a flood of powder hissed like sand onto the floor.

'Your uncle is trying to break down the door,' said Circastes. 'I suppose he thinks he has nothing to lose. He'll have a hard time getting past those heavy barrels.'

'You agreed to let Simeon go,' said Casimir. 'He can leave with Joachim and Ruth. Wake him up now. I want you to keep your promise.'

'In a moment.' Circastes nodded towards the door, and the stack of barrels came tumbling down. There was a crash and the bolt gave way. The last barrel of gunpowder toppled over and Joachim pushed through the gap, a coal shovel in his hand.

'Wake up, Simeon,' said Circastes casually, and Simeon stirred. There was a confused, exhausted expression on his face, but for the first time his eyes were sane. He looked at his hands, at Casimir, Circastes, and Joachim standing in a sea of gunpowder. Ruth was close behind, scrambling over the obstacles in the doorway. When she saw Simeon she stopped uncertainly, and lifted her hand to push away her hair.

'They're all here, Simeon,' said Circastes. 'Just as I promised you they would be. Your brother-in-arms, your lover, and your son. Only Cas is coming with me, I'm afraid. He's given me the power of his name.'

Simeon closed his eyes. 'Oh, Cas,' he said. 'I warned you. I told you not to trust him.'

'I don't trust him,' said Casimir. 'But he said he'd let you go if I gave him my name, and I had no other choice. It will be all right. I know it will be all right.' As he said the words, he desperately willed this to be so, willed Simeon to understand exactly what he had just done. He took a step towards his father. Simeon reached out a hand and laid it on his shoulder. Casimir felt a prickle of electricity, as if some last remnant of magic had discharged through him, and then the warmth of his father's touch through his wet shirt. It was real and solid, and in that moment he sensed they had both reclaimed something. In his head, he heard words distantly spoken, and felt a gentle eddy as Circastes's magic passed him by.

The magician's right hand was lifted in a gesture of power. He was holding the black wand Simeon had stolen from Ezekial Circastes, and he looked faintly foolish, as if he did not entirely understand what was happening. He had called on Casimir's name, and found there was no power in it. Casimir, who had expected this, looked at Simeon and saw realisation dawning in his dark eyes.

'Ah.' Simeon started to laugh. 'I see. Indeed, indeed, I see.'

'I gave him my name,' said Casimir simply and then Joachim burst out laughing too, for like Simeon and Casimir, he understood the trick. Though he used it for convenience, Runciman was not Casimir's name. His parents had never been married, and legally, he was a Leibnitz like Joachim and Jessica, the illegitimate son of a wild redhead who had hung out in the artillery train of the Ostermark army and run off with her brother's friend. Jessica's name was the only legacy Casimir's mother had left him, the only part of her time or memory could not efface. And the proof had gone up the kitchen chimney with his birth certificate.

Simeon laughed again and the sound made Casimir rejoice. Casimir knew Circastes had probably spoken the truth about what Simeon had done. But he alone knew that in the years since then his father had learned much and abjured more, and though the dark and twisted turnings of his life were full of regrets and mistakes and might-have-beens, if there had been no Ezekial Circastes, Simeon would never have grown into the flawed, troubled man who was his father, and whom he loved, and Casimir himself would never have been born at all.

All this passed through Casimir's head in a flash. He had not noticed Circastes creeping slowly forward to the firepot. It was Simeon who saw and lunged at him, too late.

'No!' Circastes's foot connected with the pot, kicking the coals into the mess of powder at their feet. With a sizz! the gigantic powder trail ignited and started running in circles around the floor. Casimir gave a shout and stamped at the sparks with his bare feet, but for every trail he extinguished another two sprang up, doubling at each fork in the pattern and running across the floor in effervescent circles. Then his feet flipped out unexpectedly from under him. Casimir fell backwards and started skidding across the floor on his backside. A green glow formed around his body and Circastes's hand grabbed him by the shirt collar and wrenched him in a single savage motion to his feet.

'Let me go!' The words locked in Casimir's throat. His muscles were frozen, as they had been at the top of the firework machine on Friday night. The green glow swelled around him. He smelled pine trees and snow and heard the waterfall, and then Circastes gave a yell of fury and the green light vanished abruptly. Joachim had grabbed the magician from behind and lifted him bodily off his feet, breaking his contact with the ground.

'Simeon! Do something! I can't hold him much longer!' Joachim shouted. Casimir slipped from Circastes's grip. Simeon was scrabbling at his bootlaces, but they were tied too tightly to undo quickly. He lurched to his feet. His weight came down on Casimir's bare shoulder and he shouted a single, guttural word.

A surge of power exploded through Casimir's body. He screamed and writhed but Simeon's grip only tightened, clamping down on his shoulder like red-hot metal. Again and again Simeon cried the word, the magical energy passing through his body into Casimir's, through Casimir's bare feet into the stone floor. Casimir reeled. Stars burst like fireworks in his head and his heart felt as if it were about to explode. The magic was burning him away, scouring through his body until there seemed nothing left of it but a thin wisp of flesh. Only Simeon's hand on his shoulder kept him standing.

There was a rumbling in the river passage and a blast of magic stench like the smell of electricity before a storm. Filthy river water poured into the cellar, sloshing around the walls. Ruth screamed hysterically. Dimly, Casimir saw Joachim and Circastes still struggling near the passage door and then the light went out and the cellar was completely dark.

A huge wave picked Casimir up off his feet, tearing him from Simeon's grip and bouncing him across the cellar floor. Something hit him in the chest, knocking the breath out of him. He went under and swallowed water, felt the current sucking back out down the passage to the river. Casimir found himself being dragged towards the door. A piece of wood bumped into him, and he flailed and grabbed hold of it.

'Simeon! *Simeon*!'

But with his grip on Casimir, Simeon had lost control of what was happening. Casimir could hear him shouting, but could not tell whether the words were magic, cries for help, or merely a name, repeated over and over until it cut off abruptly and there was silence.

As violently as it had arrived, the receding water began to calm. Casimir surfaced, still clinging to his piece of wood. He saw a pale glow appear on the surface of the water, a prickling of bubbles. A box of roman candles floated past him in the direction of the passage.

'*Simeon!*'

There was no reply. Water swirled past him, carrying with it a flotsam of wood, red cardboard and gunpowder. A single, dark-haired figure staggered to its feet near the cellar door. Casimir saw that it was Joachim, clinging to the firework boy like a life buoy. He glimpsed a dark shape bobbing under the water. But the glow around it was already fading and after that there was only darkness and the lingering scent of magic and gunpowder.

CHAPTER TWELVE

When the Queen's Guard raided the treasurer's cellar in the early hours of the morning they found a large number of sodden fireworks, a dozen smashed kegs of gunpowder and a sea of river water which had inexplicably flooded in and was unable to drain away. The explosives were traced to Simeon Runciman the firework maker, who was already being sought on suspicion of conspiracy and black magic. A warrant was issued for his arrest. But when the officers of the Queen's Guard went hunting for them, Runciman, his son, and the man known to have been staying with them had disappeared. No-one had seen them leave the city and an exhaustive search of their known haunts and the roads leading out of Starberg proved inconclusive.

It was not until several weeks later that the badly decayed body of a dark-haired man was discovered jammed up against the grating at the far end of the river passage. One side of the head had been smashed against a firework mortar in what the procurator's surgeon identified as the death wound. In the absence of other evidence the body was presumed to be the missing firework maker, but there was an element of uncertainty in the identification, for two other men with similar colouring were known to have been in the cellar with him on the night of the plot. The taint of magic as well as treason hung around the whole incident. On the procurator's orders, the body was taken from the Undercroft and hanged in chains as a traitor, then ceremonially burned in the market place. Later, when further information had been laid and the report was written up, more secret recriminations were ordered against another person who had left Starberg for Osterfall around the time of the attempted attack. But by then the ashes of the supposed magician were lying at the bottom of the Ling, and the whole affair, a nine days' wonder, was already beginning to be forgotten by most of the populace.

While the water ebbed in the treasurer's cellar, the celebrations whirled on inside the palace, the queen's guests in their silks and laces oblivious to the peril in which they had stood. A few people remarked on the absence of the treasurer's daughter, and many more on the news that Princess Christina had unexpectedly left the capital. Nobody paid any attention to the upheavals taking place under their feet. Even the coachmen and grooms who were the nearest to what was happening were preoccupied, drinking, or dead drunk. It was Christmas, after all, and though a coachman claimed to have heard subterranean rumblings, and a stablehand swore a bedraggled man passed him in the tunnel, it was not until much later that it occurred to them to report this. In consequence, when Casimir, Ruth and Joachim stumbled out of the cellar shortly before midnight, nobody stopped or questioned them. The world, except for them, was too busy having a good time.

After the light in the cellar had faded, there had been a great deal of confusion. Nobody could see, and Ruth, who had been washed into the stairwell by the first inrush of water, had badly injured her hand. While Casimir was not precisely in shock, he was in a state of denial, refusing to admit that his father was dead, that Circastes had won a sort of pyrrhic victory over them before vanishing. Even when Joachim fetched—stole—a lantern to prove that Simeon and the magician had, truly, disappeared, he had not wanted to leave the cellar. He sloshed around thigh-deep in the darkness, while Joachim fished for bodies and Ruth clung, onehanded, to the rail of the cellar steps. On Casimir's insistence, he and Joachim had even explored the river passage for a short distance, until the water reached the ceiling and they could go no further. But there was nothing to find. The dark human shape Casimir had seen under the glow on the water was gone.

'He must be there. I saw him, he *must* be.'

In the end, Joachim lost his temper. 'Face facts, Cas. He's not here. Or if he is, he's drowned, and there's nothing we can do. There's no point in pursuing this. If we're going to have a chance of getting away, we have to leave, now.'

'We *can't*.'

'We can. And we will.'

'I'll help,' said Ruth, and that was when they gone back to the house. Inside the servants' Christmas party, like the queen's, had reached the raucous drunken stage. They stopped at the linen room for towels and Joachim backtracked to wipe up the puddles of water they had left. Then they crowded into Ruth's little sitting room, where a small fire was still burning from earlier in the evening.

Gathering the necessaries from around the house took some time. They needed salves and bandages, laudanum, dry clothes, food, as much money as Ruth could give them, which, since her father controlled her purse strings, proved in the end to be not very much at all. Joachim demanded a razor, and retreated into an adjacent bedroom to shave off his beard. Casimir stripped off his wet things and towelled himself dry. He pulled on the ill-fitting clothes Ruth had found for him and sat on the settle. The soles of his bare feet were peeling and new pink skin showed through the scorch marks. Simeon's last magic had healed, even as it had burned through his flesh. Nevertheless, the scars would always remain to remind him of what had happened.

The door opened and Ruth came into the room. She poured a dose of laudanum from the bottle she was carrying and drank the sickly, brown fluid down.

'How's your hand?' asked Casimir.

'Hideous.' She grimaced, but the pain on her face was very real and Casimir realised only iron willpower was keeping her going. 'I think it may be broken. I shall have to have it seen to by a doctor. But it can wait. It will have to. What are you going to do now? Go to your mother?'

Casimir shook his head. 'I don't even know where she is. I guess I'll go into the army. I can mix gunpowder and operate a cannon. They won't ask too many questions when they learn that.' He thought of Simeon at seventeen, fleeing from the magician's stilt house above the waterfall, and wondered if he would ever break free from the consequences of his father's sin. Grief welled up inside him, for Simeon, for himself, so intense it blotted out almost everything else. For a moment he hardly realised that Ruth was speaking to him, far less heard what she was saying.

'Casimir, about your mother.' She said it again and somehow, this time, her words penetrated the fog of Casimir's wretchedness. 'I didn't realise. I always assumed you knew where she was. Simeon told me. She's married and living in Sluijt.'

'In Sluijt?' If Ruth had said his mother was in China, Casimir could not have had more trouble taking it in. Yet Sluijt was three hundred miles away, not three thousand. It was a difficult journey, but not an impossible one. 'What do you mean?'

'I mean, if you want to go to her, that's where she's living,' said Ruth. 'Your father told me. After she'd left him, he worried about her, and he always kept track of where she lived. I think he was trying to stop me feeling jealous by telling me she was so far away, but all he did was make me angry that he still cared enough to be concerned after all those years. Of course, I didn't know about Circastes, then. I suppose Simeon must have been using magic to keep an eye on her.'

Casimir thought of the lock of hair he had found in the guncase. 'Do you know anything more?'

'I believe her husband's a dealer in salted herring.' Ruth shot him a twisted smile. 'They have three young children. It all sounded terribly respectable. But I can't give you precise directions, or her husband's surname, just that the youngest child was called Anneke. She was born last summer, and when Simeon told me, I got really upset. After what happened to me years ago, I can't have children. But with your mother's name, and the baby's, and the husband's profession, you should be able to track them down. They sounded reasonably well-to-do, and Sluijt's not that big a place.'

To Casimir, it seemed like a miracle. He could not quite believe it: that Ruth, whom he had detested, and whose life he had worked so hard to make difficult for the last nine months, had just thrown a rope into the pit of his despair. For if his mother was not dead, or mad, or any of the terrible things he had imagined, but alive and well and married, living beyond the borders of Ostermark, then there was hope for him, too. And if he ever got over the loss of his father, if he ever came to truly understand what had happened twenty years before and over the past five days, then maybe it would be possible to forgive himself for being his father's son and fight back. Not against Circastes, for that would only reduce him to the magician's level, but against the dark glamour which Simeon had struggled all his life to reject, the magic which Circastes called power, but which in the end was only deceit and coercion, and the imposition of one human's will onto another.

On impulse, he blurted out, 'Why don't you come with us?'

'I can't. I'd be a millstone around your neck.'

'If you stay, Christina will kill you.'

'I wouldn't count on that,' said Ruth, and a note of harshness had returned to her voice. 'My father knows the procurator well. As soon as you're far enough away to be safe, I'll be making arrangements to talk with Margrave Greitz about Christina. I'm sure, between the three of us, we will be able to reach some kind of accommodation.'

The door opened before Casimir had a chance to reply, and Joachim reappeared. He had changed his wet clothes, shaved, and trimmed his hair with a pair of scissors. Without his beard he looked so different that Casimir barely recognised him.

'Are you ready?'

Casimir pulled on his boots. 'Yes.'

He picked up the bags that Ruth had put together for them and the three of them went back downstairs. Joachim disappeared to fetch something and Casimir and Ruth went out into the River Court. It was dead midnight. The lamps along the carriageway were starting to burn out. It was still drizzling rain, and as they stood on the water stairs, waiting for Joachim in front of their boat, it seemed to Casimir that Ruth looked old and worn. On impulse, he put his arm around her and gave her a swift awkward hug.

'Goodbye, Ruth,' he said. 'I'm sorry.'

Ruth clung to him for a moment.

'Goodbye, Cas,' she said. 'Try not to hold it against me.' She let him go, and Casimir climbed into the boat.

For a moment Ruth stood forlornly on the landing, but then she seemed to realise there was no point in waiting and went back up the steps. Casimir watched her disappear into the drizzle. Of them all, he realised, Ruth had gambled and lost the most. Something else besides Simeon had passed out of her life for good. She was the one who would have to make the explanations and deal with the procurator and Princess Christina. Casimir shivered. Whatever she said about doing deals with the Procurator, he did not think the princess would treat those who thwarted her kindly.

Joachim came running down the steps. The night wind ruffling his newly shorn hair. He had a bulky oilskin bundle under his arm, which he thrust at Casimir; it was flat, and irregularly shaped, and Casimir thought he knew what it was. He moved the baggage to make room for his uncle at the oars and sat in the prow with it huddled in his cloak.

He leaned over the side and loosed their mooring. Joachim pushed off. As they drifted downstream and the lights of the palace slowly faded in the rain Casimir heard, in the distance, the last bell tolling the passing of Christmas Day.

※

They travelled downriver all day, a swift current running behind them, and crossed from Soderdale into Strasland in the middle of the afternoon. Since it was the morning after a holiday, and raining, they saw hardly anyone, only a farmer securing his haystacks against the weather, and the odd solitary wanderer travelling nowhere. Shortly before sunset Joachim steered the boat ashore. The muddy banks of the Ling rose up onto a piece of waste ground. Casimir pulled their baggage into a heap on the bank and sent the boat floating on downstream. There were two knapsacks Ruth had given them, one of them stuffed with papers. There was also the firework boy. Joachim had rescued him from the cellar and, with uncharacteristic sentiment at the last moment, refused to leave him for the guards.

'He saved my life, Casimir,' he said. 'I owe you for that. Don't think I will ever forget it.'

'We can't take him with us, though,' said Casimir. 'He's too big.'

'True,' said Joachim, 'but we'll give him a hero's funeral, just the same.'

Casimir cleared the ground and together he and Joachim gathered wood to build a fire. There was not much dry kindling anywhere and the damp sticks would not light. He pulled some sheets of paper out of the knapsack and started screwing them into balls. After a page or two he realised smudges of ink were coming away on his hands. He looked more closely, and saw that it was the manuscript of *The Tyrant* which he had last seen snatched by Simeon from the kitchen fire. Ruth had obviously given it to him as a parting present.

'Here, Cas,' said Joachim. 'It's not safe to take that with us. Let me.' He scrunched the rest of the poem up quickly and poked the paper balls between the sticks. A moment later a small flame appeared in the midst of the twigs.

'Do you think Circastes survived?' Casimir asked. It was his first implicit admission that Simeon had not.

'Maybe,' said Joachim. 'I don't know. I lost hold of him in the water. I had him in my grip and then suddenly he wasn't there any more. He might have drowned and been caught in the passage, he might have escaped back to where he came from. If he has, there's no doubt he'll be back. No matter where you go, no matter who you travel with, there will always be that element of uncertainty and suspicion. But I just don't know.'

He threw the last of *The Tyrant* on the fire. Fuelled by the paper the flames raced through the twigs and pine needles and licked at the larger sticks. A few words stood out in silhouette on one of the pieces of paper, but though he tried, Casimir could not read them. The page twisted and collapsed, its cinders lifting on the hot air.

'Go on, Cas,' said Joachim. 'This is your magic, now.'

Casimir picked up the firework boy and tossed him awkwardly onto the flames. A shower of sparks flew up, and, since he had only imperfectly dried out, it was a while before he caught. But at length a bluish flame began to lick along the edge of the glossy painted curls and the cardboard cases of the coloured matches flared up and sank back into ash. Some sparks flew from the hair and the catherine wheel eyes gave a few sizzling starts and spun lopsidedly around. When the last spark had extinguished the board that was the firework boy's body caught ablaze. The flames turned green from the paint and gave the blue and crimson trousers a strange metallic sheen. Finally, that too, was gone. Casimir kicked it to ash and ground the last few bits of charred wood and paper into the mud.

'That's it then,' he said. He picked up his bags and turned his face to the setting sun, a red wintry sun that sent gleams of crimson through the bare branches of the trees.

'That's it,' said Joachim. He smiled at Casimir, and two of them went together into the darkness, leaving nothing to mark their passage except two sets of footprints, one large, one slightly smaller; and behind them on the river bank the mark of one bare foot.

I am not generally given to writing afterwords to novels, but *Fireworks and Darkness* is such a special book, and one in which so many people believed with such sincerity and passion along the way, that I thought this time I would break my normal rule and elaborate a little on its origins.

Fireworks and Darkness has had a much longer gestation period than anything else I have ever written. Simeon and Joachim, or versions of them, date back over fifteen years; the story of the firework shop and its inhabitants almost twelve. My first attempts to put it down on paper were a depressing failure, largely due to my own inexperience at that time. Yet the idea was too potent to give up on, and over the years, in between many other books, I kept coming back to it, worrying the text to pieces and reassembling it over and over again. Bits were added and thrown away, the point of view swung around like a weathercock, the age of the main character changed (at one stage I even considered changing his sex). Throughout this frustrating time the manuscript was abandoned more than once in sheer despair; but books are like politicians, for if they hang on long enough, their time generally comes. Early in 2000, in the course of one of my periodic returns to Fish Lane, I rewrote the opening chapter for what seemed like the hundredth time. Miraculously, after all those years, it came out exactly the way I had always wanted it to, and I knew then that the day of *Fireworks and Darkness* had arrived.

People who have read the novel to date have invariably been fascinated by the fireworks and at this point it seems appropriate for me to mention a book without which it could never have been written. Casimir Simienowicz's treatise on military and recreational fireworks, *The Great Art of Artillery*, was first published in Latin in 1650. I first encountered the 1729 English translation many years ago when I found a decrepit facsimile edition on the shelves of the public library I used to run. Who was responsible for the purchase of so esoteric a work I have no idea, but I was instantly transfixed by its possibilities and regret to admit that when I left the job I weeded it out of the collection. (My only excuses are that no one else ever borrowed it, and that I couldn't risk leaving it behind.) Simienowicz was the Lieutenant-General of the Ordnance to the King of Poland and a notable seventeenth century expert on artillery and firepower. Modern lovers of fireworks tend to forget that the benign shells and rockets they are used to have more sinister near relations, and not surprisingly Simienowicz's work concentrates heavily on military fireworks. Nevertheless, its lovingly detailed period diagrams and explanations of the construction of shells, rockets, perfumed water globes and set pieces provided me with most of the information I needed to bring Simeon and his profession to life (and incidentally provided the names for the two main characters).

In conclusion, several people who helped with the book need to be mentioned: my husband Peter, for giving me the precious hours in which to write it; my dear friend, Maria Letters, who unwittingly uttered a note of encouragement at a point when I was thinking of giving up; the unknown lady at the CBC Conference in Brisbane in 1996 who came up to me when I *had* given up and begged me to finish it on the strength of the first two paragraphs (I hope she finally does get to read it, and that the wait has been worth it); and my friend Linda Miller, for her ongoing help with maps and diagrams. One person, for whose opinions I have enormous respect, believed in this book far more than I did myself. Her ongoing care and interest in it over many years have done more than anything to ensure that it finally saw daylight. Finally, and most importantly, I must thank the midwives: my agent, Margaret Connolly, editors, Sandra Davies and Emma Kelso, and publisher Lisa Berryman for loving the book so much and working so hard to convince me that *HarperCollins* were the right people to publish it. I trust the end result has justified the faith of everyone who believed.

Natalie Jane Prior
April 2001

blind A firework which fails to explode.

catherine wheel A spiral shaped firework that spins around on a central pin, spitting out sparks.

composition See *gunpowder*.

cracker A small firework, usually red in colour, which explodes with a loud 'crack' and a characteristic jump.

fuse The 'wick' used to ignite a firework. Fuses are made either by rolling tissue paper around gunpowder, or by impregnating cotton cords with gunpowder grains. By joining many fuses into a 'train' it is possible to set off several fireworks at once.

girandole A type of firework like a wheel, which spins horizontally on a pole. In the past, girandoles were sometimes allowed to 'take off' like fiery flying saucers.

gunpowder The explosive agent used in all fireworks. Gunpowder is normally comprised of 75% saltpetre, 15% charcoal and 10% sulphur, though slightly different compositions are used for different purposes.

firework machine An elaborate structure forming the background for a firework display.

mortar A short-barrelled cannon used to shoot firework shells into the sky.

nails Special 'launching pads' for rockets.

pyrobolist Archaic word for a firework maker and operator; the modern term would more normally be *pyrotechnician*.

rocket The most famous firework, a rocket consists of a cardboard tube with a conical top and a long stick to stabilise it during its flight. Burning gunpowder in the tube propels the rocket into the sky until the flame reaches the firework stars in the cone and the rocket explodes. Rockets are usually launched several at a time in *flights* or *volleys*.

roman candle A stationary firework which alternates a fountain effect with single stars.

salute A firework designed purely for the purposes of making noise, often used to signal the end of a display. Also sometimes called a *maroon* from the French *marron* (chestnut), which makes a popping sound when roasted in a fire.

shell A round or cylindrical case containing firework stars, fired out of a mortar into the sky.

slow match Specially treated cord which burns very slowly, and which is used to set off fireworks.

stars The chemical material in the firework casing which produces the characteristic firework 'sparkle'.

whizz-gigs Small fireworks, often added to a shell, which shoot erratically across the sky.